THE *KAT SINCLAIR* FILES

BY MICHELLE SCHUSTERMAN

FINAL GIRL

Grosset & Dunlap
An Imprint of Penguin Random House

THIS ONE'S FOR THE GHOSTS OF YOUR PAST—MS

GROSSET & DUNLAP
Penguin Young Readers Group
An Imprint of Penguin Random House LLC

Text copyright © 2017 by Michelle Schusterman. Cover illustration copyright © 2017 by Stephanie Olesh. All rights reserved. Published by Grosset & Dunlap, an imprint of Penguin Random House LLC, 345 Hudson Street, New York, New York 10014. GROSSET & DUNLAP is a trademark of Penguin Random House LLC. Printed in the USA.

Book design by Kayla Wasil

Library of Congress Cataloging-in-Publication Data is available.

ISBN 9780448479828   10 9 8 7 6 5 4 3 2 1

CHAPTER ONE
THE HAUNTED HOUSE

Fright TV: Your Home for Horror
Press Release: January 9

SCREAM QUEEN EDIE MILLS'S DOCUMENTARY SERIES COMING THIS SUMMER

Former teenage Scream Queen Edie Mills will be producing and narrating MAGIC HOUR, a 13-episode documentary series that details her rise to horror movie stardom from 1972 to 1985.

The series will include exclusive behind-the-scenes footage from Mills's most popular films, including VAMPIRES OF NEW JERSEY and INVASION OF THE FLESH-EATING RODENTS, as well as RETURN TO THE ASYLUM and its controversial prequel. Fans will enjoy never-before-seen interviews with cast and crew, as well as stories from Mills herself about her infamous disagreements with studio heads and her experience with a stalker, the details of which she kept out of the press at the time.

MY reflection glared at me, fists clenched as if she wanted to punch through the mirror and wrap her hands around my neck. I exhaled slowly, forcing myself to relax, letting my fingers uncurl one by one. *Brush your teeth,* I told myself. *Fix your hair. Then get out.*

I grabbed the tube of toothpaste next to the sink and rolled it up to squeeze the last bit onto my toothbrush. A lot of girls probably looked at themselves critically in the mirror, especially before a date. But I'd bet none of them had a ritual like I had. Every morning for the last three weeks I'd had to force myself to face off with my reflection. Because I hated her. Because I was afraid of her. Because honestly, I'd be happy if I never had to look at her again . . . but obviously that wasn't an option.

After tying back my hair and sliding in a few bobby pins, I switched off the bathroom light and headed over to the giant, open box near the front closet. The sticker with our hotel's address in New York was peeling off in places, but I could still read the return address:

Edie Mills
3852 Sparrow Street
Chelsea, OH 43209

My chest tightened a bit as I knelt next to the box. The smell of my house, the one I'd grown up in, filled my head as I inhaled deeply. It smelled like Grandma's perfume and apple spice air freshener and Pledge furniture cleaner.

I missed that house. Kind of.

Grandma had packed the box neatly and carefully, but after a few weeks of Dad and me rummaging around inside without ever actually unpacking, it was kind of a mess. Winter clothes and boots were jumbled up with folders from Dad's home office and boring-looking mail about tax returns. There'd been a package of snickerdoodle cookies from Cinnabeth, my favorite bakery in Chelsea, but those were long gone.

There had also been a formal invitation to my mother's wedding in May. I'd mailed the RSVP back to her that day without giving myself time to think too hard about checking *Yes*. Then I'd taken a short, frigid walk to Central Park and thrown the invitation into a frost-covered trash can.

Now, I unearthed my favorite hoodie—black with dark red claw marks across the chest—and slipped it over my head. "How's the research coming?" I asked, looking around for my snow boots. Oscar was sitting at the desk in front of my dad's laptop, head in his hands like he was reading intently. His aunt Lidia, *Passport to Paranormal*'s producer, was working in their room, and Oscar had been desperate for some Internet time. When he didn't answer, I grabbed my boots and sat on the edge of my bed directly behind him.

"Hel*lo*?" I nudged his back with my toe. He jumped out of his chair and spun around, eyes wild and unfocused. I tried not to laugh. "Did you actually fall asleep in the three minutes I was in the bathroom?"

Oscar blinked, and his gaze sharpened. "No. Well . . . just for a few seconds."

I double-wrapped the laces around my boot before knotting them. "Still not sleeping well?"

He mumbled something incoherent under his breath as he sat down and pulled the laptop closer. I eyed the back of his head, wondering if I should press further. The whole *P2P* crew had spent the last few weeks together in New York after shooting an episode in Buenos Aires. My dad and Oscar's aunt Lidia, as host and producer of the show, had been busy meeting with Fright TV executives about our next few episodes, which would be the last of the second season. So I wasn't sure if they'd noticed the change in Oscar: constant yawning, dark circles under his eyes, easily distracted. When I finally asked him about it on New Year's Eve, he told me he'd been having weird dreams and waking up a lot. He didn't offer any more details, and I didn't ask. I knew Oscar pretty well by now. It always took him a while to open up about stuff.

Sometimes, though, he needed a little push.

"Nightmares?" I asked lightly, pulling on my other boot.

Oscar shrugged without looking at me. "They're not nightmares."

"You said weird dreams," I said. "I assumed you meant bad weird. So . . . nightmares."

"No, I meant they're . . ." Oscar broke off, yawning widely. He turned around when I stood up, and stared at my boots in surprise. "Where are you going?"

I wrinkled my nose. "To that paranormal museum? To check out the thoughtography exhibit? Remember, we talked about it last night . . ."

His expression cleared. "Oh, right."

"Seriously, what's going on with you?" I asked. "Did you

get some bad news or something?"

"No, it's . . ." Oscar stopped and shook his head. "It's hard to explain. Later, okay? You're gonna be late."

I glanced at the time on the laptop screen. "Yeah, all right."

My gaze fell on a stack of papers between the laptop and the mirror. Fright TV had renewed *Passport to Paranormal* for a third season after our Buenos Aires episode's great ratings. The contract they'd given my dad had been sitting on our desk for almost two weeks now. Oscar and I shared a glance before I slid it toward me and flipped to the last page. At the sight of the still-blank line, I sighed.

"He still hasn't signed?" Oscar said, brow furrowed. "Why?"

"Eh, he's probably just waiting for his agent to approve it." I ignored the twinge in my stomach and pushed the contract back to where Dad had left it. "Maybe they have to negotiate some stuff."

"Maybe," Oscar replied. "But I'm pretty sure Roland and Sam turned theirs in a week ago."

"Huh." I grabbed my puffy gray winter coat off the armchair. "I'm sure Dad'll turn it in soon."

"Hope so."

I swallowed hard as I zipped up my coat. I'd been trying not to stress about that unsigned contract, but every morning that I woke up to find it still on our desk made it more difficult. And it bothered me that Roland Yeske and

Sam Sumners, *P2P*'s parapsychologist and medium, had already turned in their contracts. Dad loved hosting *P2P*. He loved his job. So why hadn't he committed to another season yet? He couldn't possibly want to move back to Ohio . . . could he?

I could just ask him. I *should*. But I was too afraid of what his answer might be.

"Did he decide what to do about your house yet?" Oscar asked suddenly. I cringed, glancing over at the box from Grandma. The day it arrived Dad and I called to thank her, and it turned out she had some news. Good news. A documentary series about her horror movie star days. Moving to L.A. to "get back into the business." *Great* news.

Selling the house we rented from her. Not-so-great news.

She wanted to give Dad a chance to buy it before putting it on the market. I could tell Dad had been just as floored as I was. He asked if he could have time to think about it, and she said there was no rush. Afterward, Dad and I just stared at each other.

"Well," I'd said. "It's not like we really live there anymore."

"But we still need a home," Dad had responded. "A home base. Between seasons."

Between seasons. He'd said that, but he still hadn't actually agreed to host season three. On the other hand, he hadn't given Grandma an answer about the house yet, either.

"No," I told Oscar. "But I mean, even if he buys it, that

doesn't mean he's not coming back to the show. We need a place to live when we're not traveling, obviously."

"Yeah." Oscar looked like he wanted to say more, but just turned back to the laptop. "Anyway. Have fun at the museum."

"Thanks."

His voice turned a little sly. "Tell Jamie I said hi."

I shot him a look, willing myself not to blush. "I will. Hey, where's my camera? It was right here by the TV."

Oscar frowned. "I didn't touch it."

I turned slowly, my eyes darting from the TV to the desk to the little table by the window. Then I spotted a flash of silver on the armchair, just behind the cushion. "Aha." I tucked the Elapse into my pocket, ignoring a familiar sense of unease. This had been happening a lot over the last few weeks—my camera, my homework, all kinds of items turning up in the wrong place. I kept trying to convince myself I was just being forgetful, but it was getting to the point where that was almost as unsettling as the other option: Someone, or some*thing*, was moving them.

After double-checking my coat pockets for my gloves, I headed down the hall to the elevator. I could worry about Dad and the house and why he hadn't signed that contract later.

But right now, it was time for my second date with Jamie Cooper.

CHAPTER TWO
WE'RE ALL
MADDER HERE

P2P FAN FORUMS
Season 3 Finale Gossip!

Maytrix [admin]
Word on the street is Fright TV's booked a guest star for the finale of *P2P* next month. Anyone have any thoughts on who it might be?

AntiSimon [member]
Bernice!! I hope, anyway. Jack's a great host but I really miss her. And the crew's in NYC right now—she works at the natural history museum there.

spicychai [member]
if it's a former host, my bet's on emily

AntiSimon [member]
Uh, pretty sure she's locked up. Also pretty sure you're joking, because why would they bring back someone who LITERALLY ATTACKED THEM.

YourCohortInCrime [member]
Ratings.

presidentskroob [member]
sorry Simon, I know for a fact it's not Bernice. (and YCIC, there is no way they'd bring that loony bird back, give me a break)

AntiSimon [member]
How do you know it's not Bernice? And hey, where's beautifulgollum? Her predictions are usually right on track. Haven't seen her post in a while.

skEllen [member]
OMG THEY WOULD NEVER LET EMILY NEAR MY PRECIOUS SAM AGAIN!!!1!!!

WHEN it snowed a few days after we got to New York, it was kind of magical. Like being in one of those miniature Christmas villages set up in the department store windows, surrounded by cotton ball fluff. But a few weeks later . . . well, it was kind of gross. Along the curbs and sidewalks, the shoveled snow had hardened into dirty gray slush. It was frozen solid, and I could see piles of trash bags trapped inside like flies in amber.

Not so magical.

I pulled my hood over my head and quickened my pace as I turned onto West 96th Street. The bitter wind cut right through my gloves, and shoving my hands in my coat pockets only helped a little. Not for the first time, I wished the crew had just decided to stay in Argentina over the holidays.

Except not really, because Jamie wasn't in Argentina.

I was walking so fast, I almost missed the sign for Madder's Museum of the Paranormal. It was hanging over an otherwise nondescript glass door sandwiched between a gelato shop and a really expensive-looking boutique that apparently sold only the kinds of caps worn by old men and newspaper boys in movies set in the 1930s. Slipping a little on the icy sidewalk, I pulled open the door and hurried inside.

For a second, I thought I'd accidentally walked into someone's home. All the museums I'd ever been to were spacious, usually with a giant foyer that split off into several halls. This looked more like an apartment—and a pretty small one, too. Except instead of sofas and chairs, it was filled with shelves and glass cabinets holding all sorts of creepy stuff: old dolls with cracked porcelain faces; jars filled with murky liquid; skulls and bones that might've been fake, but it was hard to tell. I spotted a stained wooden Ouija board and made a mental note to tell Mi Jin to check out this place before we left New York.

"Kat!" Jamie waved from the back of the room. Next to him, a petite middle-aged woman with bright blue hair and a *Ghostbusters* T-shirt beamed at me.

"Kat Sinclair!" she called, skirting around a cabinet and hurrying toward me. "Oh wow, it's *so* cool to meet you!"

I blinked in surprise as she grabbed my gloved hand and shook. "Um, hi!"

"Carrie Madder. My mom owns this place, but she's retiring next month so I'm basically running it now. I've been reading your blog since the beginning," she rambled, helping me out of my coat and hanging it on a rack by the door. "I'm on the *P2P* forums all the time, too. We miss having you on there, by the way!"

I smiled, trying not to cringe. I'd stopped hanging out on the fan forums last month when this troll kept posting horrible things about me. Horrible things that I knew weren't true, but that I still thought about every day.

"That's so cool!" I said, hoping my face wasn't red. "I've never met someone from the forums in real life before. What's your username?"

"Presidentskroob," Carrie replied. "Man, you and Oscar are so great. I've always loved this show, but it's even better with you guys on it."

Now I was definitely blushing. "Thanks!"

Jamie joined us. "Carrie was just telling me there's supposedly going to be a guest star for the finale," he told me eagerly. As usual, his smile set off a ridiculous amount of fluttering in my stomach. "Have you heard anything?"

"No, nothing." I smiled back at him, resisting the urge to press my frozen hands to my flaming-hot cheeks. We'd spent a lot of time together the last few weeks, but always with his sister, Hailey, and Oscar. This was the first time it was just the two of us since our first date to a graveyard in Buenos Aires. Well, just the two of us and a really chatty museum curator. Part of me wished Carrie wasn't around, but another part of me was relieved. I loved hanging out with Jamie, but calling this a *date* made it differe

Exciting and a little bit nerve-racking.

"Well, if the host's daughter and the network VP's son don't know anything, maybe it's really just a rumor," Carrie was saying. "That's a bummer."

"Not necessarily," Jamie said. "My dad pretty much never tells us anything about the show."

"But Kat's a cast member," Carrie said, grinning at me. "They wouldn't keep her in the dark, right?"

I pictured my dad's unsigned contract and shrugged. "I don't know. They might, to be honest."

"Well, if there *is* a guest, I know for sure it's not Bernice Boyd." Carrie lowered her voice, despite the fact that we were the only ones in the museum. "I saw her last time I went to the natural history museum and asked." She snorted. "A few fans think it's Emily Rosinski. As if they'd ever do that, no matter how wild the ratings would be."

At the mention of Emily's name, goose bumps broke out on my arms. "She's in a psychiatric hospital," I said, keeping my voice even. "There's no way."

"Oh, I know," Carrie said hastily. "Sorry, I shouldn't have brought her up."

A slightly awkward silence fell, quickly broken by Jamie. "So, where's all the thoughtography stuff?"

Carrie's face lit up. "In the back room! Follow me."

She led the way around the shelves to a corridor. Jamie took my hand and squeezed, and we smiled at each other. My frozen fingers finally started to thaw. But I couldn't help getting chills as I pictured Emily the last time I'd seen her. Knocking Oscar unconscious, pulling out her knife, forcing me up the twisting staircase to the prison guard tower, and—

"Ta-da!" Carrie exclaimed, and I jumped, jerking my hand out of Jamie's grip. He gave me a concerned look, which I pretended not to see. "Our psychic photography exhibit. I helped curate all of this—thoughtography's kind of an obsession of mine."

I gazed around the room, which was much smaller than the other one. The walls were covered in framed photos: some yellowed newspaper clippings, some black-and-white, and even a few color Polaroids and prints. In the corner, a small TV sat on a card table, topped with a VCR. Static played silently on the screen.

"So Jamie told me you guys did a little research on thoughtography already," Carrie said, gesturing for us to check out the pictures hanging near the door. "I've tried to curate only pictures that haven't been debunked . . . which is pretty hard to do, because most of the ones out there are fake." She tilted back her head, glancing at the ceiling. "You should see the number of boxes I've got upstairs, all filled with what I was told were psychic photographs that turned out to be bogus. It's really easy to do." Carrie grinned at me. "Well, you probably know that already."

"What?" I asked, startled. "Why?"

"Because you're a photographer," she said. "You know,

you can mess with the exposure, the printing . . . although, I guess it's a little different with digital cameras. Have you ever played around with analog cameras?"

"A little," I said. "A really long time ago, though. My, um . . . my mom's a photographer. She brought me to a darkroom a few times in elementary school."

"Do you remember much about developing?"

I frowned. "A little bit . . . you put the negative in the enlarger and set a timer for how long you want it exposed to light, then put the print in the developer, then a . . . um, a stop bath? I think that's what it's called. And then a water bath—no, the fixer, then the water bath—and then you hang it up to dry."

"Exactly." Carrie pointed to a small framed black-and-white photo behind me, and I turned to look. "So what do you think went wrong there?"

Jamie leaned closer, too. The slightly blurred picture featured an older man in a suit sitting in a chair in what looked like a study or office. He had no beard, but thick, dark hair covered the sides of his face and extended down to his chin. His expression was stern yet exasperated, as if posing for this photo was a massive waste of his time. Behind him, a bookshelf was just visible next to an open door. Beyond that, the corridor was dark, save for a blur of white.

"A ghost?" Jamie asked immediately.

I shook my head. "Nope. Whoever printed the photo just underexposed that part, that's all."

"Exactly!" Carrie said. "But in 1896, this guy published a whole paper about what he called evidence of psychic photography. You'd be amazed at how many people tried stunts like this back then. Even though they were almost all proven to be frauds, a lot of people still totally bought it."

Jamie looked half-amused, half-embarrassed. "I probably would've," he admitted.

"Because you *want* to believe," I said. "There's nothing wrong with that."

He smiled at me in a way that made my heart thump a bit faster, and I hoped Carrie didn't notice the blush creeping up my neck. "So why'd you include this one if you know it's fake?" I asked her.

"As an example," she replied, leading us over to the next photo. "So that people will understand the real thing when they see it."

"Whoa," I whispered, stepping closer to study the picture. It was taken at the foot of a grand wooden staircase, at the top of which stood a woman in a silk gown with a high waist and lace sleeves. She was smiling in a posed sort of way, seemingly unaware of the other, transparent woman huddled at the bottom of the stairs, this one in a dark, long-sleeved dress with full skirts. Her features were blurred, so all I could make out were two dark spots for eyes and a thin line for a mouth.

"So, Kat," Carrie said. "Any idea how you could fake that?"

"Photoshop?" Jamie joked, and she laughed.

"Not really a thing a hundred years ago."

"Long exposure?" I suggested, pointing to the woman in the silk gown. "With a slow shutter speed, she would have to hold her pose for several seconds while the photographer took the picture." I pointed to the other woman. "If *she* was walking down the stairs at the same time, she'd appear all blurry and transparent in the photo."

Carrie raised her eyebrows. "Wow. I think you remember more from your mom than you give yourself credit for."

I tried to smile, even though my skin prickled uncomfortably at the mention of my mom. "Thanks."

"But," Carrie went on, "how do you explain this?"

She tapped the photograph hanging next to it. The two were almost identical, but taken from slightly different angles, as if the photographers were standing a few feet apart at the base of the stairs. The woman in the silk gown stood in the same pose, the same small smile curving her lips. But the other woman wasn't there at all.

"These were taken at a mansion up in Harlem in 1912," Carrie said. "Two photographers. The one who captured the image with the ghost, his family owned the place. He'd grown up believing it was haunted by his great-grandmother, and as he was taking this picture of his niece, he was thinking about her. Really *focused*. That's why she appeared in his photo, but not the other. At least, that's the story his son gave me when he donated this to the exhibit."

"*Awesome*," Jamie said fervently.

16

"I know there's no way to prove this is a real psychic photograph," Carrie said. "But there's one other detail that pretty much convinced me. Any guesses?"

Jamie and I studied the picture again. "Oh!" Jamie exclaimed. "Her dress—the great-grandmother's dress."

Carrie beamed. "Exactly!"

I must have still looked confused, because Jamie continued. "This was taken in 1912, but her dress has petticoats, a high collar, long sleeves. Totally different than what the niece is wearing."

"But very much in fashion in the mid-eighteen hundreds," Carrie finished. "When great-grandma here still lived in the mansion."

I exhaled slowly. "Oh. Okay. That's . . . that's pretty cool."

"*Really* cool," Jamie added, his eyes sparkling. I couldn't help but grin at how into this he was. I believed in ghosts, but I still tried to stay skeptical until I saw proof. Jamie was always ready to believe.

Carrie led us through the rest of the small exhibit, giving us the story behind each photo and why she believed it was real. She showed us the footage of a séance captured on VHS; it was only fifteen seconds, so we watched it probably a dozen times. A dark figure appeared in the shadows right at the twelve-second mark, then vanished. No one at the table seemed to notice it, and as Carrie explained, the woman behind the video camera had claimed to have projected the image from her mind.

It was outlandish and ridiculous and to be honest, a few months ago I never would've believed any of it for a second.

But now? Maybe I did. Because I'd done it myself.

I'd never shown anyone the flash drive currently tucked safely in my backpack back at the hotel. The footage it contained of a figure moving behind me in the mirror as I practiced being on camera seemed just as outlandish and ridiculous as anything in this exhibit. But I'd been there. I'd been thinking about this, the other version of me. The Thing. And it had appeared.

I couldn't prove it any more than the woman who'd taken this séance video, or the man who'd captured a photo of his great-grandmother in the mansion. So who's to say they weren't telling the truth, too? Maybe they were. Or maybe they were crazy.

Maybe *I* was crazy.

Psychic photography was an explanation for that footage, and that was a relief. But I hadn't been *trying* to do it . . . so why had it happened? The idea that I might have projected the Thing there without meaning to kind of freaked me out.

The distant sound of bells jangling pulled me from my thoughts. "Be right back!" Carrie said, hurrying out of the room. Once she was gone, Jamie turned to me.

"So, do you think this one's—"

"I think I created a ghost," I blurted out, surprising both of us.

Jamie's eyes widened. "You . . . what?"

I'd told Oscar about the Thing back in Brussels. And when we got to New York, I'd told him about what really happened in Buenos Aires—that somehow, I'd created an artificial ghost based on this other version of me. The version my mother had always wanted: a *pretty little princess* kind of daughter. I hadn't seen the Thing since that last night in Argentina, but I *felt* it around me constantly. Hovering just outside of my peripheral vision. Lurking in the corners of every mirror. Breathing down my neck, as it had most of my life. When Dad first got this job with *Passport to Paranormal*, I'd thought traveling around the world was my chance to get the Thing out of my head.

I'd never meant to do that *literally*. Now it was with me in a very real way.

Oscar had believed me. But that didn't mean he believed in the Thing. I mean, part of me even wondered if I was hallucinating—a thought just about as terrifying as the Thing actually being real. I knew Oscar had to be thinking the same thing. We were both skeptics, after all.

But Jamie was a believer. And right now, I needed someone to believe me. Even if I didn't quite believe myself.

So I took a deep breath. Then I gave him the short version, glossing over all my embarrassing issues with my mother and focusing on the fact that I'd created a ghost version of myself that was now haunting me. Jamie's expression remained serious the entire time, not a trace of worry or skepticism.

"And I don't know how to get rid of it," I finished. "It's not . . . you know, *possessing* me. Nothing like that. It's just . . . with me. All the time."

"You have video of it," Jamie said slowly. "You projected it onto a video, just like this?" He gestured to the séance playing on a loop behind us, and I nodded.

"Yeah." I winced, sure he was about to ask if he could see the video. I wasn't exactly thrilled at the thought of him watching me stammering and rambling anxiously on camera, trying to get rid of my stage fright. But instead, he said:

"If you can project it, maybe you can *control* it."

"What?"

The bells jangled again, and I heard footsteps as Carrie headed back to the exhibit. Jamie stepped back—somehow we'd ended up standing really close—and grinned at me.

"I have an idea."

Rumorz
All the celebrity gossip you need (and then some)!
**POLL: Which former host would YOU most like to see guest star
on *Passport to Paranormal?* by Shelly Mathers**

1. Carlos Ortiz. Miss those dimples!
2. Bernice Boyd. Her historical insight actually made the show
educational!
3. Emily Rosinski. Give me the drama!
4. Other: _____

Comments (1)
[The Real Kat Sinclair]
You won't care about any of these idiots once you meet me.

"I'M sorry!"

I gasped, sitting upright in bed. Blood rushed in my
ears as I gripped the sheets, my palms sweaty. The clock
read 8:28—two minutes before my alarm was set to go off.
I had a vague memory of Dad's alarm going off a few hours
earlier.

Throwing the comforter aside, I hurried over to the
desk and stared at the laptop, my dad's notes, his calendar,

my camera. What was I even looking for? I pressed my fingers to my eyes, trying to think. I'd had a dream that I'd done something to make Dad upset. I'd woken myself up apologizing to him. But for what?

Exhaling slowly, I gazed around the room. Nothing out of the ordinary. It had just been a dream. A nightmare.

I showered and dressed quickly, pulling my hair back and brushing my teeth without looking in the mirror. It wasn't until I grabbed my camera that I realized what was missing from the desk.

Dad's contract.

Relief flooded through me, and I actually laughed out loud. He must have signed it and brought it to the Fright TV meeting this morning. Finally.

I grabbed my coat and headed to the lobby to meet Oscar, feeling ten times better than I had when I'd woken up. No more stress dreams about Dad leaving *P2P* and making us move back to Ohio. Maybe I'd actually get some decent sleep tonight.

The Montgomery apartment building took up almost half a block and loomed high overhead, all sparkling white stone and gray marble gargoyles. A doorman stood stiffly at the entrance, pulling the gold-and-glass door open after we gave him our names.

"The Coopers are expecting you."

"Holy . . ." Oscar trailed off, gazing around the lobby. "I

knew they were rich. But I didn't know they were *this* rich."

I shoved my hands into my coat pockets. "Maybe because Jamie and Hailey don't, you know . . ." I stopped as a woman descended the grand staircase at the far end of the lobby. She looked like she was on her way to a photo shoot: thigh-high leather boots, gray sweater dress, and a dark yellow cloak with an almost laughably enormous hood. Oscar and I watched her cross the lobby, the heels of her boots clacking loudly.

"Because they don't look like that?" Oscar finished.

"Yeah. I bet their mom does, though." Over two weeks in New York, and we still hadn't met Jamie and Hailey's mother. Apparently, being the editor-in-chief of *Head Turner* fashion magazine meant you spent a lot of time traveling and attending fancy events without your kids. Hailey had complained about their parents' busy work schedules on more than one occasion. Although at least their dad brought them on some of his trips.

Oscar shook his head. "Man, I wish they'd asked us over sooner. We could've spent the last two weeks hanging out here instead of at the hotel."

"Yeah," I said, pressing the up button on the elevator. Honestly, I'd thought it was kind of weird Jamie and Hailey hadn't invited us to their apartment until the vlog came up. It was probably just my imagination, but it was almost as if they hadn't wanted us to see where they lived for some reason.

As we waited, Oscar glanced around and pointed to another elevator on the opposite wall. The door was an ornate brass gate, and instead of a digital panel showing the floors there was a brass sign sticking out just over the doors that said "Floors: 1st to 28th" in old-fashioned script.

"That must be it," he said. "The haunted one."

It had been Hailey's idea to record the next episode of our vlog, *Graveyard Slot*, in her own building. She swore the manually operated elevator the building's owners had kept during renovations was haunted by the ghost of its first elevator operator. Oscar and I had agreed to film here, because it was a good story. And more importantly, all of the other supposedly haunted venues we'd looked into—theaters, bars, hotels—had wanted to charge us a fee to film an investigation there. A really, really high fee.

"Well, yeah," Mi Jin, the show's intern, had said when Oscar and I griped to her about it. "You don't think all the places we've filmed just let us do it for free, do you?"

Luckily for us, the manager of the Montgomery, had said yes when the Cooper kids had asked if they could take some video of the building's elevator for a vlog, free of charge. Then again, you'd have to be a serious miser to charge your tenants to film their own elevator in a place like this. The Coopers' apartment probably cost thirteen times whatever our rent was for the house in Chelsea.

Oscar and I rode up the elevator in silence. He kept yawning while I checked my backpack for the tripod. I thought about asking if he was still having trouble sleeping, but decided not to. Clearly he was, and I didn't want to make him cranky right before we filmed. I had enough anxiety of my own to deal with—or at least I would once I turned on my Elapse. Ever since I dropped it in a pool at the site of a residual haunting in Brazil, it had carried the same feelings of nervousness and panic that lingered around that campsite. Not exactly a feature I wanted in a camera, but the Elapse had been a gift from my grandma. And it was the nicest thing I'd ever owned. Even if I could afford a new one—which I definitely couldn't—I hated the thought of giving up this one.

"Okay, 2206 . . . there it is." I led the way down the hall, suddenly nervous for a whole other reason. I knew Mr. Cooper wasn't home because of that meeting at Fright TV . . . but what if Mrs. Cooper was here? I knew exactly two things about Jamie and Hailey's mom: She worked in fashion and she hated Ouija boards. Which pretty much guaranteed there was no way she'd like me.

Not that I should care. But Jamie and I were . . . well, friends. Friends who went on dates. Had he told his mom about that? What if he introduced me as his girlfriend? I wasn't, at least not yet . . . was I? Did I *want* to be?

The door flew open, and a woman exclaimed: "Kat! Oscar! *So* nice to finally meet you!"

I gaped at her. Which was really rude, but I couldn't help it. This was *not* how I'd pictured Mrs. Cooper. She was wearing torn jeans and a green flannel shirt. No makeup, no jewelry. She looked young—like, maybe even Mi Jin's age, although that wasn't possible. Definitely way younger than Mr. Cooper, though.

And she had brown skin, like me.

That's what was making my brain short-circuit. Because my mom and grandma were white, and I'd been on the other side of this situation a hundred times. Watching people blink in polite confusion, looking back and forth between us, trying to work out if we were *really* related. Sometimes it was funny to watch them act all awkward. But it got old.

I didn't want to do the same thing right now. So I stuck out my hand and said, "It's nice to meet you, Mrs. Cooper."

Her eyes widened. Then she burst out laughing.

"No, I'm Rachele!" she exclaimed. "Or, wait—oh, you were kidding! Jamie keeps talking about how funny you guys are. Mrs. Cooper," she said, still giggling. "Yeah, as if. Come on in!"

I exchanged a glance with Oscar and was relieved to see he looked as confused as I was. We'd known Jamie and Hailey for about three months now, and I was pretty sure they'd never mentioned anyone named Rachele.

We followed her inside, and Oscar coughed loudly—to cover his surprise, I assumed. I had to consciously close my mouth before Rachele saw me gaping again. Because I'd never been in an apartment like this.

It wasn't particularly large, but the massive windows,

high ceilings, and mirrored cabinets gave the impression of a ton of space. The wood floors were polished so much I could see my own reflection, and the sofa and armchairs were so bright-white I found it hard to believe anyone had ever actually sat on them. A massive rectangular chandelier hung overhead, hundreds of strands of crystals catching the sunlight streaming in from the windows. I spotted the kitchen on the other side of the room and was momentarily surprised at how small it was . . . and then I realized it was a bar, complete with a sink, a small refrigerator, and a shelf lined with all sorts of bottles, along with fancy-looking glasses in all shapes and sizes.

"I think the kids are in Jamie's room," Rachele said, already heading down the hallway to the right. "Make yourselves at home!"

I waited until she was out of sight before turning to Oscar. His eyes were bugging out of his head.

"What?" he said, gesturing around. *"What?"*

I giggled. "So I guess your place in Oregon isn't like this?"

"Um, *no?*" Oscar pointed at the wall of windows. The view was overwhelming; we were high enough to see all the way across Central Park to the buildings on the other side. "This is . . . I mean, is *your* house anything like this?"

I snorted. "No. It's bigger, but it's . . ." I pictured the scratchy blue carpet, the beige couch we'd had since I was six, the wallpaper along the staircase that was so scuffed up that the diamond pattern was indistinguishable in some places. "Well, kind of a dump, compared to this. Although weirdly enough, I *do* have that exact chandelier in my bedroom."

Oscar's lips twitched, but he nodded solemnly. "What a coincidence. I've got that statue in my bathroom." He pointed to a large figurine on the fireplace mantel of a woman riding a horse. "Right on top of the toilet . . . wait."

There was a second of silence as we both realized the statue-woman was completely naked. Then we started laughing. The silent kind, where you're trying so hard to hold it in, tears leak out of your eyes instead. I heard footsteps and swatted Oscar's arm, trying to get myself under control, too.

"You're here!" Hailey squealed, flying across the room and tackling me in a hug. As soon as she pulled away, I wiped my eyes and cleared my throat.

"It's only been two days since—*oof!*" Oscar winced as Hailey threw her arms around him. My rib cage ached in sympathy. Hailey's hugs were no joke.

"Hey, guys," Jamie said. He and Rachele joined us, and although he was smiling, I couldn't help noticing he looked a little more subdued than usual. Like he was nervous.

"Hi!" I said a little too brightly, purposefully turning away from the statue. "Your apartment is *amazing*."

"*Really* amazing," Oscar added, his voice cracking a bit. Giggles bubbled up in my throat again, and I pressed my lips together, horrified. I couldn't stand the thought of hurting

Jamie's and Hailey's feelings. Not that Oscar and I had said anything mean about their apartment . . . but somehow, I knew that if they'd heard what we'd been saying, they wouldn't find it as funny.

Jamie's cheeks were pink. "Thanks. So, you guys ready?"

"What's the rush?" Rachele exclaimed. "Oscar, Kat, do you guys want a drink? Snack? We've got carob bars—they're gluten-free—and I think there's some prosciutto rolls in the fridge . . ."

"That's okay," I said quickly. Jamie's expression was even more awkward now, and even though I wasn't looking at Oscar, I had the strong sense he was trying to hold back more laughter. Probably because I was, too. "We should really start filming. But thanks!"

"Any time!" Rachele followed us to the front door. "Well, I hope I get to spend more time with you guys later. Between the show, your blog, and everything Jamie and Hailey have told me, I feel like I know you both so well!"

She waved, then closed the door, leaving the four of us out in the hall.

"She's really nice," Oscar said as we headed for the elevator. "So, um . . . who is she?"

Now even Hailey looked a little uneasy. "She's our nanny."

"Oh! I didn't . . ." I hesitated. A nanny? I thought that was only for really little kids. But saying that out loud seemed rude.

Oscar broke the awkward silence. "Like Mary Poppins?" he joked, and Jamie and Hailey looked even more uncomfortable. Oscar cast me a worried look as Jamie pressed the down button for the elevator. "I was just kidding..."

"You guys never mentioned her before," I said lightly. "She seems really cool!"

"She is," Jamie replied, not quite meeting my eyes. "Our parents hired her a few years ago, when things started getting really busy at both their jobs. They're not home a lot."

"It probably seems so dumb to you guys," Hailey added, stepping onto the elevator. "You're both traveling all over the world, doing all this crazy stuff, and our parents don't even trust us to make our own dinner or get to school by ourselves."

"It's not dumb!" I said quickly. "Besides, my dad can be really strict, too. Remember what happened in Crimptown, when I saw Sonja? Dad was so mad after that, he and Lidia said we couldn't even watch them film the next episode."

"But you did anyway," Hailey said, her expression equal parts admiration and jealousy. "You snuck out of the hotel and went all the way out to that prison, even though you knew Emily was probably there. You guys are really brave."

Now Oscar looked uncomfortable. "And really stupid. She attacked us."

"And you should've heard the huge lecture my dad gave me after that," I said. "He almost quit the show, he was so upset!"

"Yeah, Aunt Lidia was seriously considering making me move back in with my other aunt," Oscar said, making a face. "Which would've meant going back to my old school. Ugh."

Jamie finally looked up. "But instead, they put you both *on* the show," he pointed out with a grin. "So now it's your actual job, sneaking around haunted places."

I laughed. "Okay, true—but we're literally not allowed to take one step away from the group without an adult coming with us."

The elevator doors slid open. Hailey led the way toward the manually operated elevator across the lobby, Oscar right behind her. Jamie tugged my arm, and we hung back.

"Did you tell Oscar the plan?" he asked. To my relief, he didn't look embarrassed anymore.

"Not yet," I said. "He needs to focus on hosting, and trying to contact the doorman's ghost. If I can't do this thoughtography thing, this still has to be a decent episode. I'll tell him when we're finished."

After we'd left the museum, Jamie had suggested I try projecting the Thing into the video for *Graveyard Slot*. He figured if I could control it, then that meant I could get rid of it. Neither of us was sure exactly *how*, but we'd worry about that later.

"Oscar! Kat!"

The four of us stopped and stared at the woman stalking across the lobby, another half a dozen people hurrying along in her wake. Behind them, the doorman was watching closely, his eyes narrowed.

"Do you know her?" Jamie whispered, and I shook my head. She was tall, blond, way too tanned for January, and totally unfamiliar. Beaming, she stuck out her hand at Oscar, who shook it, looking completely bewildered.

"Shelly Mathers, *Rumorz*. It's *so* good to finally meet you!" Her teeth gleamed like Tic Tacs.

Oscar's expression cleared. "Oh! Hi, Ms. Mathers!" Already, I could see him turning on his TV-show personality. While I kind of hated being on TV, Oscar loved it. He'd even done a phone interview with Shelly back when we were in South America.

"Oh, it's just Shelly, please." She gripped my hand next, and I winced. "Kat Sinclair, at last. And you must be Jamie and Hailey Cooper!"

"Yeah." Jamie kept his hands in his pockets and took a protective step in front of his sister. He regarded Shelly with a cool, almost suspicious look that surprised me. Usually Jamie was nice to pretty much everybody.

Shelly, apparently unfazed, gestured to the people behind her. They all looked younger than her, maybe in college or even high school, and I realized a few of them were wearing *P2P* hats or shirts. "Apparently I wasn't the only one who couldn't resist meeting you all. I assume you don't mind?" she added, aiming her blinding smile at me. "You *did* mention on your blog you'd be filming the next episode of *Graveyard Slot* today. Can't blame your fans for taking the opportunity to meet you!"

I forced myself to smile back, but my stomach was tense. "I didn't mention *where* we were filming, though. How'd you find us?"

"Oh, it was easy enough to find you." Shelly pulled out her smartphone, tapped it a few times, then held it out to record us. "So! Can you give us a little inside scoop? What kind of spooky stuff happens here at the Montgomery?"

She was looking at Oscar, as was everybody else. He was the host of our vlog, while I did all the behind-the-camera work. And normally, Oscar ate up this kind of stuff. But now he looked uncertain.

"Well," he said, glancing hesitantly at Jamie. "See that elevator over there? It's the original, built in 1910 and preserved during this building's renovation a few decades ago." His voice grew stronger, more confident. "In 1947, there was a massive blizzard. Some of the gears froze, and the elevator operator was trapped between the top two floors. Before they could rescue him, the cable snapped and the car plummeted all the way to the basement. According to"—he faltered for a moment, glancing at Hailey—"some tenants, the operator's ghost still haunts the elevator."

A few of the fans had pulled out their phones, too, and I

realized they were all recording and taking photos. My skin prickled, and my palms felt damp. I hated being on camera. And these people seemed perfectly nice, but it was a little creepy knowing they'd read about this on my blog and then come here just to see us. Not to mention Shelly. I shot a nervous glance at Jamie, but he was still glowering at the reporter. Hailey had stepped away from him and started gesturing at the doorman, who nodded and pulled out his walkie-talkie.

Shelly didn't notice. "*Fascinating* story," she was saying. "Can't wait for the vlog! So I hear you're taking off for China next?" Oscar nodded, but Shelly went on before he could say anything. "And then the finale will be in South Korea. Rumor has it you've got a big guest star planned. Any chance you can give my readers a little hint as to who that might be?"

"We honestly haven't heard anything about a guest star," Oscar said. "Sorry." I squinted at him; he'd gone pale, his TV personality totally vanished.

"Aw." Shelly pouted in a way she obviously thought was cute. "Well, feel free to drop me an e-mail if you hear anything. And speaking of rumors, Kat, is it true your dad isn't coming back next season? The old host curse back in action, huh?"

Suddenly, all eyes—and phone cameras—were on me. Anxiety washed over me in a quick wave, and I clenched my fists.

"Actually, my dad turned in his contract to Fright TV this

morning. Did you *hear* that rumor? Or did you *start* it?"

My voice came out way more aggressive than I'd intended. But I couldn't help it. I'd never really liked Shelly Mathers's articles, but this was different. She was cornering us into an interview without even asking if we wanted to give one. There was no way she'd ever do that with Dad or the rest of the crew . . . because they were adults.

They would be *furious* when they found out she'd done this. Somehow, that realization made me feel a little braver.

Shelly's eyes hardened, although she kept smiling. "Oh, Kat, I'm *so* glad to hear that. We'd hate to lose Jack Sinclair, wouldn't we?" she added over her shoulder, and several of the fans nodded fervently. "So I guess we don't need to worry about the fact that he's currently discussing joining *Live with Wendy* as co-host?"

I just stared at her, mouth hanging open. *Live with Wendy* was a local talk show that filmed in Cincinnati—only about an hour from Chelsea. But Dad hadn't said a word to me about a job offer. Shelly was just making stuff up. She must be.

Except . . . why would a reporter in New York know anything about a talk show back in Ohio?

"He's . . . I . . . no." My tongue felt too thick in my mouth. "He's not leaving *Passport to Paranormal*."

Eyebrows raised, Shelly waved her phone. "Good to know. I'll quote you on that."

"Um . . ." I shook my head, vaguely panicked. "I'd rather not—"

"Excuse me," a voice interrupted, and we all turned to see a security guard standing behind the fans. She was a good head shorter than Shelly, but stared her down with a look so fierce, the fans around her all took a step back. Shelly smoothly pocketed her phone as she turned around.

"Yes?"

"I'm going to have to ask you all to leave," the security guard said. "Only tenants and their guests are allowed in this building."

Shelly gave a little laugh that made the hairs on my arms stand on end. "Oh, fine. I'm sure I'll catch them later." She winked at Oscar before following the fans to the exit, where the doorman was waiting. Oscar's charming on-camera smile was back, but he watched her warily. One of the fans, a teenage girl about my height wearing a T-shirt that said #TeamSamland, lingered behind. She glanced hesitantly at the security guard before holding out a glossy photograph and a Sharpie to me.

"Sorry, I just . . . I was wondering if I could get your autograph?"

My face burned. "What? Seriously?"

"Yeah!" She waved the photograph, which I recognized from the *P2P* website. It was a promo shot the cast had taken on the boardwalk in Rotterdam, right after Dad had joined. "I've been watching *Passport* since it started, but it's *so* much better with you and Oscar. And I love your blog!"

The security guard still had her eye on Shelly's retreating

back, but she made a gesture at me that said "go ahead." I took the paper and pen, unable to think of a reason to say no. "Oh. Thanks." I scribbled my name on the bottom right corner, and she bounced up and down on her toes.

"Thank you so much! Oscar, can I get yours, too?"

"Sure!" Oscar said eagerly, taking the photo and marker from me. "What's your name?"

"Laurie!"

I watched as Oscar wrote *For Laurie: Believe! Oscar Bettencourt* in big, sprawling script, and rolled my eyes. Of course Oscar had perfected an autograph. I wondered if he'd practiced it before.

"Hey, Kat," Laurie said. "What did you mean about meeting the real you?"

I blinked. "Huh?"

She took the photo and marker from Oscar. "You know, that comment you left on Shelly's poll this morning? The one about who people wanted to see as a guest star on the finale? Something like 'you won't care once you meet the real me'?"

"Sorry, I don't—"

"Okay, that's enough," the security guard interjected, and Laurie blushed.

"Sorry! Thank you! It was great to meet you both!"

She hurried across the lobby and out the doors, where her friends were waiting. Shelly was nowhere in sight.

"Thanks, Kim," Jamie said to the security guard, who smiled at him.

"No problem. I'm going to have to tell your parents about this, okay?" Kim glanced at the door again. "What was that reporter's name again?"

"Shelly Mathers." Hailey made a face. "From *Rumorz*. I liked her better before I met her in person."

I glanced at Oscar, who had gone silent after Laurie left. He was the one who'd kept reaching out to Shelly, agreeing to her interviews. But clearly this little incident had made even him uncomfortable. After Dad and Lidia found out, there was no way they'd ever agree to more *Rumorz* interviews.

My stomach clenched as I remembered something else. I'd told Shelly my dad definitely wasn't leaving the show. *I'll quote you on that.* But what if it wasn't true? What if she published it, and it turned out my dad actually was taking some job in Ohio?

No way, I told myself firmly. He would never keep something that huge from me. And besides, his contract had been gone this morning. It was fine. I had nothing to worry about.

"Kat? Ready?"

Jamie's voice interrupted my thoughts, and I realized Oscar and Hailey were already heading for the elevator. "Oh! Yeah, coming."

I pulled out my Elapse as I walked, trying to focus on the Thing. But I couldn't stop thinking about what I'd told Shelly Mathers. If she was going to publish what I'd said, I had to warn my dad. Which meant we were finally going to have the conversation we'd been avoiding about our plans after the season finale.

"It'll be fine," I told Oscar as we hurried down the street, my voice muffled in the scarf I'd wrapped around half my face. The wind had picked up, and every bit of exposed skin stung from the cold. "Once I get it edited, it'll be a good episode."

Oscar shrugged noncommittally, but I could tell he was disappointed. Our attempts to record any sort of paranormal activity in the Montgomery's elevator had been a total bust—not so much as a flickering light. Even Oscar was off his game, stumbling over the backstory and asking the elevator operator the same question twice in a row. The confrontation with Shelly Mathers must have gotten to him.

It had definitely gotten to me. I barely thought about the Thing the whole time. No chance of any thoughtography, not when I was so busy worrying about talking to my dad.

"Hey, why'd you look all freaked out when Shelly mentioned a guest star?" I asked, and Oscar's head jerked up.

"What? No I didn't."

"You did," I said, giving him a weird look. "And you do right now, too. What's going on?"

He pressed his lips together. "I don't know. Do you think there really is one and we don't know about it?"

I shrugged, pulling open the door to our hotel. "Maybe. So?"

"Well, some of the fans in the forums think maybe—"

"Kat."

My dad stood in the center of the lobby, and at the sound of his voice, I jumped.

"Hi!" I said, pulling off my hat and scarf. "Everything okay?"

But clearly it wasn't. Dad's arms were crossed, his mouth was set in a thin line, and—I squinted—yeah, his cheek was twitching. His patience timer, Grandma called it.

My heart began thumping painfully against my rib cage. Somehow, Shelly must have already published something in the last two hours. This was exactly why Oscar and I weren't supposed to give interviews without someone else from the cast present.

"She ambushed us," I blurted out. "She showed up at Jamie and Hailey's building—a security guard came and kicked her out! It wasn't our fault, we—"

Dad's expression rapidly changed from upset to alarmed. "Wait, hold up. What are you talking about?"

"Shelly Mathers," I said. "From *Rumorz*."

"She didn't even ask if she could interview us," Oscar added. "She just started recording and asking questions. Just for a minute or two, then the security guard made her leave."

Dad's jaw tightened, and for a moment he didn't say anything. "Oscar, Lidia's up in your room," he said at last. "Will you go tell her about this, please?"

Oscar nodded and headed for the elevators. Dad turned to me.

"I'm sorry, Kat." His voice was softer now, and my shoulders relaxed. "Fright TV assured us the media knew its boundaries when it came to you and Oscar, but apparently not. We'll take care of this so it won't happen again."

"Thanks." I swallowed hard. "There's something I need to tell you, though. She said . . . she said she heard a rumor you weren't coming back next season, so I—I know I shouldn't have said anything, but she even mentioned the host curse and . . . and well, that's all garbage, right? So I told her you were definitely coming back."

Dad didn't say anything, just watched me. And now I was really nervous, because the patience timer had stopped, and I couldn't read this expression. Not angry. Not alarmed. Not confused. But something close to all three.

"I mean, you *are*, right?" My voice rose a little. "The contract was gone this morning, so you turned it in. Right?"

Dad's forehead wrinkled, and he pulled a plastic bag out of his pocket. "Well, that's what I wanted to talk to you about. I got back to our room after the meeting and found this under my pillow."

I peered in the bag. It was filled with shredded paper, all ripped up like homemade confetti. And there were words printed on each strip in small black font. Words like *network* and *warranties* and *agreement*.

"Is that . . . your contract?" I stared up at him. "You tore it up? Why did you do that?"

Dad squeezed his eyes shut briefly, like he had a headache. "Come on, Kat. You're too old for games like this."

"What?" My head buzzed with confusion, and I had a flash of déjà vu. My dream. I'd dreamed about this last night, about Dad being angry with me for doing something.

For *destroying* something.

"You think I did that?" I whispered.

"Well, I didn't," he replied. "Housekeeping didn't visit our room today. And no one else has a key. Who did it, if it wasn't you?"

I gazed at the shredded contract, my eyes and throat burning. It hadn't been on the desk when I'd woken up. Whoever shredded it had done it after Dad left, while I slept just a few feet away. And I knew who it was. *What* it was.

The Thing wasn't just lurking in mirrors anymore. It was up to something.

Dad was still watching me. I felt trapped. There was no lie I could tell that he'd believe—but would he believe the truth?

"It was . . ." I paused, swallowing. "I think it was a . . . ghost. No, listen," I went on hurriedly when his brows arched in disbelief. "I've been noticing that my stuff keeps getting moved around, like my camera, my notes for history lessons. And I've . . . I've seen it."

"Seen what?"

"Um . . ." I couldn't do this. Dad was already looking at

me like he feared for my sanity, and I hadn't even gotten to the crazy stuff yet. "Like a . . . figure. A ghost. I don't know!" I yelled, suddenly frustrated. "Just something, okay? It's following me and messing with me and it tore up your contract, not me!"

All traces of anger and frustration were gone from Dad's face. "Kat, honey," he said, his expression so filled with concern it made my throat tighten. "I didn't realize . . ." He leaned down so he was at eye level with me. "We've experienced some scary stuff since we joined this show, haven't we? And I know you love being scared, but . . . maybe it's been a little too much."

"What?" I gaped at him. "No, it's not that, I'm not *scared*." But the wobble in my voice betrayed me, and tears started to spill over. "I'm not scared," I repeated anyway. "That's not what this is about."

"We don't have to keep doing this," Dad said gently. "We can go back to Ohio, Kat. It's okay."

I couldn't believe this. "Are you trying to punish me?"

Dad blinked and straightened up. "I'm trying to *help* you, Kat."

"By threatening to make me move back to Chelsea?" I wiped my eyes furiously. "You know I want to stay with the show. I'm not scared, and I didn't rip up your—"

"Jack?" We turned to see Jess in the elevator, holding the doors open and looking at Dad expectantly. "I've been texting you—that conference call starts in a minute."

"Be right there!" Dad faced me again, lowering his voice. "Kat, stick around the hotel for now, okay? Maybe get some rest. I'll check in on you in an hour."

I didn't trust myself to speak, so I just nodded. Dad headed for the elevator, and I sank down onto the lobby's sofa.

Dad hadn't been angry, and he hadn't thought I was lying. That should've been a comfort. But he thought I was *scared*. Like being on a ghost hunters show actually *frightened* me . . . not just that, but that I was so freaked out I thought a ghost was haunting me.

He thought I was crazy. And I hadn't even told him the full truth about the Thing. If he thought the solution to me seeing a ghost was to send me back to Ohio, what would he do if I told him I'd created a ghost that was another version of *myself*?

Have me committed, probably. I didn't want to lie to my dad. But the truth hadn't worked, either. I'd have to fix this without his help.

Trouble was, I had no idea where to begin.

CHAPTER FOUR
NIGHTMARE ON
CLOWN STREET

Post: The Montgomery Elevator
Comments (19)

As most of you probably know, tomorrow the *P2P* crew is heading off to Beijing. I'll have a post up soon about where we're filming, but for now, here's two clue words:

1. Demonic.
2. Bridge.

(Yeah, it's going to be amazing.) (Virtual candy corn for anyone who guesses right in the comments!)

In the meantime, we spent the holidays in New York City, which was really fun and REALLY cold. Oscar and I thought this would be a great place to film the third episode of *Graveyard Slot*. There've got to be plenty of haunted places in this giant city, right? Turns out there are—and one of them happens to be the home of Fright TV vice president Thomas Cooper. You probably remember his kids, Jamie and Hailey, from our last episode about Brunilda Cano. They took us for a ride down to the basement of the Montgomery building on a century-old manually operated elevator, where we attempted to contact the operator who died there nearly seventy-five years ago.

A quick note: For the first time ever, we got to meet a few fans of *P2P* in real life today! One of them mentioned a comment supposedly from me on a recent *Rumorz* poll. I just wanted to let you guys know that it's not me—just some random person using the name "The Real Kat Sinclair." No idea what that's about.

Anyway, hope you enjoy the video! More soon from Beijing.

HAILEY stood framed in Oscar's doorway, hands on her hips and a scowl on her face, like an adorable sixth-grade supervillain out for vengeance.

"There *is* a guest star."

There was a clattering sound from the bathroom, and I frowned. "Oscar? You okay?"

"Fine," came his response. Maybe it was my imagination, but his voice sounded a little wobbly.

Jamie and Hailey didn't seem to notice. "How do you know?" he asked his sister before popping another Cheeto into his mouth.

"I heard them in Roland's room," Hailey said. "Jess was talking about doing a special segment on the finale, and Lidia said they'd have to cut one of their usual segments, and your dad said 'Which one?' and Lidia said she didn't know because they'd never had a guest star until now."

Oscar stepped out of the bathroom carrying an armload of toiletries. "You were eavesdropping?" he asked, heading to his suitcase and dumping the bottles inside. He sounded normal now, but his lips were a thin line.

Hailey rolled her eyes. "Look, if they don't close their door all the way then it's not a *secret* meeting. Anyone walking by could overhear." She flopped down on the bed next to Oscar's suitcase. "And you're missing the point. *There's a guest star.* And they didn't tell you guys!"

"So?" Oscar said, and Hailey sighed loudly.

"Aren't you mad? You're part of the cast, too!"

"Oh, right." Oscar nodded. "I'm furious. Roar."

His deadpan tone made Hailey giggle. Jamie nudged my leg with his foot.

"It doesn't bother you?"

I made a face. "Honestly? I can't blame them. I couldn't even keep my mouth shut about my dad staying on for next season around Shelly Mathers. And it looks like I was wrong, too."

"He didn't say he's leaving," Oscar said quickly. "He just said he's still thinking about it."

My talk with Dad after his conference call yesterday had not gone well. According to him, I'd been "not acting like myself" ever since we left Buenos Aires. He thought the news about Grandma selling the house, and the fact that he hadn't made a decision about whether we should buy it, had made me frustrated with him. Which . . . okay, yeah, it had. Still. It was pretty insulting that he thought I'd have a meltdown like that.

He hadn't helped matters by telling me he hadn't signed the contract yet for a reason. "The contract is for the whole season," he'd said. "A year. I took this job mid-season because Bernice broke her contract and I needed work. This is a longer commitment. Between this and the news about the house . . . I just need some time to think about it."

I hadn't bothered asking him about *Live with Wendy*.

47

The possibility that Shelly Mathers knew more about Dad's career than I did would just be more fuel for my anger.

"What about your contracts?" Jamie set the bag of Cheetos on the desk and looked from me to Oscar. "Has the network given them to you yet?"

"Nope," Oscar said. "They're holding off on mine and Kat's until her dad signs his."

I sat up straight. "Wait, what? Why are they keeping yours? You can still be on the show even if Dad and I leave."

Oscar shrugged. "Actually, I don't think the network would want that. Remember, that's how it was when they first asked us to join the cast. It was both of us or nothing."

He said it lightly, but guilt washed over me, anyway. He was right. If Dad decided to leave the show—even though I *knew* he loved this job—there was a good chance Oscar wouldn't be part of the cast anymore. And he *loved* being on TV. It wasn't fair.

"You're all coming back," Hailey said confidently. "I bet your dad's just trying to get more money, Kat. That's how negotiations work."

I didn't have the heart to tell her what Dad had said. "Yeah, you're probably right."

Hailey started speculating on the guest star again, with Jamie and I throwing out increasingly absurd suggestions to make her giggle. But Oscar stayed uncharacteristically quiet while he packed.

Something about this whole guest star thing was

bothering him. And I had a feeling it wasn't just that the rest of the cast was keeping it a secret from us.

A knock sounded on the door, and Mi Jin poked her head in. "Rachele's downstairs," she said, then laughed when Hailey let out a little wail of despair.

"I can't believe you guys are going to Beijing, and we have to stay in stupid New York and go to stupid school on Monday."

I laughed, but a pang of sadness hit me. I wasn't ready to say goodbye to Jamie and Hailey yet.

Mi Jin gave her a sympathetic smile. "Don't worry, kiddo. I'm sure we'll work out another trip with you guys when we start shooting season three!"

"Yeah, next fall, which might as well be a hundred years from now," Hailey grumbled. Then she took a deep breath and faced Oscar, lifting her chin like a soldier heading off to battle.

Oscar's expression was serious. "See you in a century," he said solemnly, and Hailey cracked a smile.

"You'd both better e-mail us every day!" she cried before launching herself at Oscar, who stumbled back into the wall. I'd barely had time to stand up before Hailey's arms were around me next, squeezing my ribs with a ridiculous amount of strength for a girl with such skinny arms.

Oscar gave Jamie a quick hug, then headed to the door with Hailey. I smiled at Jamie, suddenly feeling shy.

"I wish you guys were coming with us," I told him.

"Me too." He paused, biting his lip. "I'll miss you."

A warm feeling filled my chest. "I'll miss you, too."

Jamie stepped forward, and I hugged him tightly. Then, without giving myself a chance to think about it, I kissed him on the cheek.

He grinned at me, his face dark pink, and started to say something. But then Mi Jin called from the hallway: "Elevator's here! Come on, guys!"

"Video chat when you get there?" Jamie asked, and I nodded.

"Yeah."

He slung his backpack over his shoulder, then took my hand, and we headed to the elevator.

That night, I pretended to be asleep when Dad came into our room. The whole contract thing, combined with saying goodbye to Jamie and Hailey, had left me feeling pretty blah. Even knowing the show *had* booked a guest star and no one had told Oscar or me bugged me more now that I'd had time to think about it. Dad didn't trust me with anything, apparently. Not enough to tell me about the show, or his job offer in Ohio, or even what he was thinking about doing with the house. Didn't I get a say in this? I was a cast member. I had a blog. I contributed to the show. This was my life, too.

I listened to the sound of the shower running, trying to think of a way to say any of that to Dad. But he already thought I'd torn up his contract in some sort of meltdown.

Anything I said now would probably just come off as more immature whining.

Then there was the other thing. *The* Thing. Knowing that it had been creeping around my room that morning while I lay right here, unconscious, was going to make it kind of hard to sleep.

The water stopped, and a few minutes later, Dad emerged from the bathroom. I buried myself deeper under the comforter as he rummaged around the closet. At last, he turned off the light and climbed into his bed. Before long, his chain-saw snores started up. It was comforting, actually. A reminder that if the Thing showed up, I wouldn't be alone.

Maybe if it did, I could wake up Dad and prove to him I wasn't losing my mind.

All night, I drifted in and out of vague dreams about being trapped in a small room, jerking awake each time and staring around the room, looking for a skulking figure in the shadows. When Dad's alarm went off at 5:00 a.m., I was torn between relief and wanting to cry.

Forty-five minutes later, I entered the lobby to find Oscar sprawled on the couch, looking as exhausted as I felt. He squinted at me through red-rimmed eyes, groaning when I flopped down next to him.

"Same," I mumbled.

We sat in silence for the next five minutes while Dad and Jess checked everyone out at the front desk. Through the glass entrance, I saw Roland pull up in one of our rental cars, followed by Sam in the other.

Yawning, I got to my feet, slung my backpack over my shoulder, and grabbed my suitcase. Oscar did the same, and I followed him across the lobby. The doors were flanked by two enormous potted palms, and I noticed the leaves trembling a bit on the one on the right. We'd almost reached the doors when a clown with blood dripping from its mouth leaped out and grabbed Oscar by the shoulders.

"GOTCHA!"

My shock only lasted about half a second, because I recognized Mi Jin's combat boots and purple hoodie. But Oscar *screamed.*

Not a fake scream, like he usually did when he and Mi Jin pranked each other. The real kind, the kind that sounded like it was ripped out of someone's gut through their throat against their will. The kind someone makes when they really think they're about to die.

Everyone in the lobby whirled around. Oscar dropped his bags and staggered away from Mi Jin, his face white. She pulled off the clown mask.

"Whoa!" she exclaimed, eyes wide. "Hey, sorry! I was just goofing around . . . You okay?" She took a step forward and reached for him, stopping when he flinched. "Oscar, seriously. Are you okay?"

We all stared at him, even the concierge behind the desk. Breathing heavily, Oscar looked around. Then, without a word, he snatched up his bags and pushed through the door so hard it slammed into the outside wall.

Mi Jin's mouth was open, and she looked from me to Lidia over by the front desk. "I—I'm really sorry!" she said. "We do this kind of stuff all the time; I don't know why he . . ."

"He's just tired." Lidia watched Oscar toss his bags into the trunk of the second car. "Hasn't been sleeping well. Don't worry about it, I'm sure he's okay." But I caught a glimpse of her expression as she turned back to the concierge, and she definitely looked worried. For a moment, I wondered why she wasn't going after him. But Lidia knew Oscar even better than I did. And I knew enough not to push him to talk when he clearly wanted to be alone.

I pulled my suitcase over to Mi Jin. "It sure doesn't seem like he's okay," she whispered, running her hand over her shaved head. "God, I've never heard him scream like that. And he looked . . . he really looked *mad* at me."

I didn't say anything, because she was right, but agreeing would probably only make her feel worse. And when I slid into the back seat of the second car next to Oscar, he was leaning against the window with his eyes closed, like he was asleep. But I could tell he wasn't.

No one said anything about the incident during the drive to the airport. Or during the long baggage check lines or security. It wasn't until everyone had bagels and coffee and chocolate milk and we'd camped out at our gate that I sat down next to Oscar and said:

"Tell me about these nightmares."

He blinked, picking a piece off his cheddar bagel and not meeting my eyes. "What?"

"You said you're having weird dreams. You're not sleeping. You get startled easily—and not just with Mi Jin, I've noticed it before. It's like you're . . . you're paranoid, or something. And . . ." I paused, waiting until he finally looked up at me. "And I know what that feels like. So tell me about it, and maybe I can help."

Oscar didn't say anything for several seconds, and I waited for him to tell me to leave him alone. Then his left eye twitched, and he rubbed it, sighing.

"Okay." He glanced around, lowering his voice. "I'm not having nightmares, because I'm not sleeping at all. It happens when I'm awake."

"What does?"

"It's like . . ." Oscar paused. "Like a daydream, but I can't control it, I'm not *trying* to think about it. It just plays over and over in my head on a loop. But sometimes there's little differences. Sometimes she has the chair, but sometimes—"

"She?" I interrupted. "Who's she?"

He blinked, his eyes flickering around nervously. "Emily."

Something cold and heavy settled in my stomach like a stone.

"When she jumped out of that cell, I saw her coming, but not fast enough to—to react. Protect myself. She hit me with a chair, knocked me out . . . and I can't stop picturing it.

But sometimes she doesn't attack with a chair. Sometimes it's a knife, or a gun. Sometimes it's nothing, and she just grabs me by the throat and—"

Oscar stopped abruptly, closing his mouth. He lifted a shoulder as if to say, *you get it.*

And I did. I'd had nightmares about Emily, too. About her attacking Oscar, about her pulling her knife out when we were in the guard tower, about her running toward Sam and me not being able to do anything to stop her.

But the more that time passed, the less I thought about her. For Oscar, it sounded like it was getting worse.

"Okay," I said slowly. "And that's why you can't sleep? Because you can't stop ob—thinking about it?" I stopped myself from saying *obsessing,* even though that's what Oscar was describing.

He nodded. "And that's why I acted like an idiot when Mi Jin jumped out from behind that plant."

"You didn't act like an idiot," I said immediately. "You were scared. You have a reason to be." He rolled his eyes, and I leaned closer. "No, seriously. We both do. We were attacked by a stalker. She literally knocked you unconscious. It was scary as hell, and maybe . . . maybe that's something you don't just get over really fast."

"Or get over at all," Oscar said dryly. "It's worse now than it was right after the whole thing happened. Especially when every time I get on the forums, everyone's talking about Emily being the guest host for the finale."

"That's obviously not going to happen."

"I know, but just seeing her name is like . . ." Oscar made a face, then sighed. "Maybe it's a good thing we might not come back next season. How am I supposed to go on paranormal investigations when I freak out over someone mentioning Emily? Or scream at the sight of a stupid clown mask?"

At his mention of next season, I felt a stab of guilt yet again, but ignored it. He did have a good point. Chewing my lip, I let my gaze wander over the other cast members. Dad and Jess were sitting close together, watching something on Dad's iPad. Lidia was on her phone, finger pressed to her other ear, brow furrowed. Mi Jin had her laptop out and was typing furiously. Sam had dozed off with his head on Roland's shoulder, and Roland was reading a paperback he'd bought in the airport's bookstore. The title looked really long and dull; I could only make out the words *Clinical* and *Human*.

"You should tell Roland."

Oscar frowned at me. "What? Why?"

"Because he's a therapist. No, seriously," I said when Oscar wrinkled his nose. "That's what he did before the show. He had patients, and a lot of people go see a therapist because something happened to them. You know, something traumatic. And I know Roland's sarcastic and weird sometimes, but he's really good at this kind of thing."

"Have *you* talked to him about stuff like this before?"

"Yeah, I talked to him about my parents' divorce a little." I grinned. "And back when we first met, I told him I didn't like you. And he told me it was because we were too alike . . . which was true." Oscar rolled his eyes again, but his lips curved up a tiny bit. "But seriously, I think he'd have some good advice for you."

Oscar looked over at Roland, and so did I. He looked up from his book, eyebrows arched questioningly.

"Can I help you?"

I glanced at Oscar, then shrugged. "I was just saying that your book looks really boring."

Roland sniffed. "I'll have you know that this chapter on third generation cognitive behavioral therapy techniques is a literal roller coaster."

Before I could reply, a voice came over the public address system.

"Flight 3366, with nonstop service to Seattle, will begin boarding in a moment."

With a loud groan, Roland elbowed Sam. "Wake up, sunshine. You've got two flights and twenty hours of flying to get your beauty sleep." Sam stared around blearily, his black hair sticking straight out of the left side of his head, and Roland pulled him to his feet. Oscar and I stood, too, picking up our bags, and I stared at him expectantly.

"Well?" I asked in a low voice.

"Okay," Oscar said at last. "Yeah. I'll talk to him when we get to Beijing."

CHAPTER FIVE

ALL WORK AND
NO PLAY

P2P FAN FORUMS
Jack Sinclair confirmed for season 4!

Maytrix [admin]
Just saw this article on *Rumorz* by Shelly Mathers. She ran into
Kat in NYC, who confirmed her dad's definitely in for next season.
Phew!

The Real Kat Sinclair [new member]
Shelley Mathers is a liar. My father and I are moving back to Ohio.
I can't wait to leave this stupid show and go home for good.

YourCohortInCrime [member]
ROFL what

AFTER almost twenty-four hours of travel, I was pretty much
delirious. I kept nodding off during our drive through
Beijing, my head jerking forward every time the car lurched
to a stop. By the time I woke up the next morning, I only
remembered the trip in flashes: Green-and-yellow buses.
Frost-covered rickshaws. Glass skyscrapers. An enormous
hotel with signs in both Mandarin and English. Key card.
Bed. Pillow. Face-plant.

I sat up slowly, my head still thick and foggy with sleep. The blinds were closed, but I could tell it was light outside. Dad was sitting cross-legged on the bed next to mine, his laptop screen giving his face a bluish glow. He smiled at me as I grabbed the glass of water on the night table and gulped it down.

"Morning. Well, afternoon, almost."

"Ugh." I set down the empty glass. For a few minutes, we sat there quietly. Dad was reading what looked like the itinerary Lidia had e-mailed to all of us before we left. I just watched him, thinking. About his shredded contract. About his reluctance to sign it. About what Shelly Mathers had said. His other job offer. The one he hadn't told me about.

I couldn't keep being angry at him for something I didn't even know he'd done. So I took a deep breath and said:

"*Live with Wendy.* Is it true?"

Dad looked up, his mouth slightly open. "I'm sorry?"

"Shelly Mathers said that show *Live with Wendy* asked you to be cohost. In Cincinnati. Did they?"

His face tightened. "Yes. And I'd love to know how some *Rumorz* reporter found out about it. They're keeping that search a secret until they fill the position."

"So I guess they've forbidden you to tell me, then." I winced at how whiny that sounded. But I had a right to be hurt. Or at least, I thought I did.

Apparently, Dad disagreed. Because instead of looking

contrite or apologetic, he closed his laptop and turned to face me.

"Kat, I didn't tell you because I haven't decided whether or not to accept the offer yet. And despite what you apparently think, this is *my* decision to make, not yours."

Stung, I just stared at him for a few seconds. "But . . . but if you take it, that means we're moving back to Ohio."

"Yes, it does."

"But . . ." Anger was quickly replacing my hurt feelings. "But that's my decision, too, isn't it? I'm a cast member—shouldn't I get a say in whether or not I leave?"

Dad sighed. "Believe me, I know you want to stay. But I'm the parent. I need to do what's best for you—best for both of us."

"And that's moving back to Chelsea?" I threw the sheets aside and stood up, trembling. "You love this job, too! What's this really about? You still don't trust me? Or you think it's too dangerous? Because—"

Ping! I stopped, and Dad and I both glanced at his phone on the night table. It was a text from Jess that just said *FYI*, followed by a link.

I crossed my arms, silently fuming as Dad tapped the link. But a second later, my righteous anger dissipated as I heard my own voice coming through the phone's speaker.

"Actually, my dad turned in his contract to Fright TV this morning. Did you hear *that rumor? Or did you* start *it?"*

"She actually posted *video* of me?" I cried, hurrying over

to look. "Can she even do that without permission?"

"It wasn't Shelly Mathers," Dad said. His voice was way too calm and even. "It was a fan. He took this video on his phone while Shelly was talking to you, then tweeted it."

The video played again, and my stomach turned over. It wasn't the whole conversation—just the clip where I snapped. I remembered how frustrated I'd been, but still, I was surprised at how *furious* I looked. Fists squeezed at my sides, arms straight, leaning forward slightly like I wanted to hit Shelly. Dad closed the browser abruptly and tossed his phone on the comforter.

I swallowed. "You're mad at me."

He took a deep breath. "No. I'm disappointed, and confused, as to why you said what you said. Especially after tearing up my contract."

"I didn't—"

"But I'm not mad at you." Dad paused, squeezing the bridge of his nose, and I pressed my lips together. "I'm mad at Shelly for ambushing a bunch of kids. I'm mad at myself for not being there to do something about it. I'm mad that when my daughter's not being attacked by psychopaths in an abandoned prison, she's being harassed by trolls online and reporters in real life. It's—"

"Trolls?" I interrupted, my face suddenly hot. "How did—I mean, I haven't been . . ."

But I stopped, because I could tell from Dad's expression that he knew. Somehow, he knew about the person who'd spent most of December leaving horrible comments on my blog. Comments I'd deleted as soon as they'd popped up— but only after screenshotting and saving each one to read over and over again later. Torturing myself. Making myself believe that all the awful things he said about me were true. Oscar was the only person I'd told, and he'd immediately deleted all of the screenshots from my phone.

"Oscar told you?" My voice came out hoarse and scratchy.

Dad's face softened. "No, Mi Jin did. Don't be angry at her—it was the right thing to do."

I didn't respond. I wasn't angry that Mi Jin had told him, because she didn't know about most of the comments. Just the first few. Which, frankly, were the kindest ones. I couldn't imagine how upset Dad would've been if he'd seen the ones that came later. They hadn't been just insulting. They'd been . . . degrading.

"Kat, why didn't you tell me?" Dad waited, and when I stayed silent, he sighed. "You told Oscar, you told Mi Jin. I just don't want you to think you can't come to me, too."

"I . . . I thought you'd make me get rid of my blog," I said at last. That was true, but it wasn't the real reason. I'd been . . . *ashamed*. Mi Jin only knew about the troll because she saw his first comment before I deleted it. Jamie knew because the troll had left another comment about me on the forums. But I'd never told him or Mi Jin how bad things had gotten. It was too humiliating.

The only reason I'd told Oscar was because I knew he'd

been through the exact same thing.

Dad sighed. "Kat, we've had this talk. A few times, actually. If there's even the *slightest* chance you're in danger—"

"It was just a stupid troll!" I blurted out. "I wasn't in *danger*; this wasn't like with Emily."

"Not just the online harassment." Dad tapped his phone. "It's happening in real life now, too. Reporters, fans, videos of you circulating online . . ."

I stood up again. "That wasn't my fault!"

"I know," Dad replied grimly. "It was my fault. You're my responsibility. I told you, I'm not angry with you. I'm angry with myself." He was quiet for a moment. "That's why I'm seriously considering Wendy's offer."

"What?"

"It's a great job," he said. "Great pay. An established show that's not under constant threat of cancellation. And less work, to be honest—I do love this show, especially working with Jess again, but it's a twenty-four–seven job. How often do you and I get to spend time together doing anything that isn't *Passport* related? Maybe . . . maybe that's why you're acting out."

"But—no, I'm not—"

"And it's *home*," he went on, as if I hadn't interrupted. "We could buy the house. You could go back to Riverview— Trish and Mark would be thrilled, right?" Dad cleared his throat. "And you'd be able to visit your mother and her new family more often. I really . . . I really think this might be what's best for you. And that's my first priority."

My face was burning, my hands were shaking. But I forced myself to keep my voice as calm as his. "And I don't get a say in this at all?"

"I already know you'd choose to stay with the show." Dad paused, shaking his head. "Although, maybe I don't know that, since you still haven't explained why you ripped up my contract."

A weird, harsh laugh escaped me. "I *didn't*."

"Then who did?" Dad watched me carefully, and I opened and closed my mouth a few times. "Kat, I can tell when you're keeping something from me. And it seems to be happening more and more lately. What aren't you telling me? If you're really telling me you didn't do it, I—I want to believe you. So just tell me, whatever it is."

I closed my eyes and imagined saying it. *Dad, last month I thought I was possessed and I tried to exorcise myself. But what I ended up doing was exorcising the Thing. The other daughter, the one Mom wants me to be. I created an artificial ghost that's an alternate version of myself, and now it's terrorizing me. It tore up your contract, and I don't know what it will do next.*

That would be the end. Dad would think I'd lost it, really lost it. He'd take me back to Ohio tomorrow. Put me in therapy. Hell, maybe even put me in a mental institution.

I *couldn't* tell him.

"Nothing," I whispered. "I don't know what happened to your contract."

Dad closed his eyes, and my heart sank. He didn't believe me. And for good reason.

"I'll let you know when I decide what to do about this job offer," he said quietly, opening his laptop again. "You'd better get ready quick if you want breakfast—the buffet closes in half an hour."

I didn't trust myself to speak, so I just nodded. Somehow, I made it to the bathroom before the tears spilled over.

CHAPTER SIX
THE THING ON THE BRIDGE

Post: The Yongheng Bridge
Comments (34)

Wow, I guess those two clue words were too easy! AntiSimon, Hailey, and presidentskroob (hi, Carrie!) all get virtual candy corn.

We're heading out to the Yongheng ("Eternity") Bridge north of Beijing this afternoon. It's too cold here for us to camp out overnight, so we'll be doing most of our filming in the early evening, right after the sun sets.

This bridge looks amazing, and I can't wait to check it out. It's about five miles long, and it winds around the sides of the mountains. In some places, it connects one cliff to the next— and the tallest section is over 1,000 feet high! The clouds hang particularly low over this mountain range, which means that even during the day, a lot of the bridge is shrouded in mist. And on some parts, we'll be INSIDE the clouds.

But that's not the creepiest thing about this bridge. It's the site of a demonic haunting. Construction on the bridge took twice as long as planned because workers insisted they felt a presence with them, hidden by the clouds. Some sort of force. It whispered to them, howled at them—even tried to PUSH them off the bridge! But unlike all the other places we've visited, there's no story about someone who died here, no ghosts looking for revenge or anything like that. Whatever's haunting this bridge was never human.

That's the legend, anyway. I didn't believe in ghosts when I joined Passport to Paranormal, and I do now. But I'm still a skeptic! We'll see what happens tonight . . .

I pretended to sleep during most of the drive through the mountains, occasionally peeking through the window to take in the view. The fog grew thicker and thicker, and soon I could only catch glimpses of sky and rocks and grassy hillsides through the haze.

Dad sat up in front next to Jess, helping her navigate as she drove. As usual, they were chatting animatedly about the area, its history, the architecture of the bridge . . . but I couldn't help thinking Dad sounded a little subdued.

It just didn't make sense. I understood him worrying about me, and I totally got why he was upset about the whole Shelly Mathers thing. But all that stuff he'd said about how much work this job was? That wasn't Dad at *all*. He loved working. Back in Chelsea, he'd get antsy after just one day off if we didn't have plans to keep him busy. And he worked overtime at *Rise and Shine, Ohio!* a ton, coming up with ideas for new segments, trying to get bigger celebrities as guests.

I'd gone over our conversation a hundred times in my head. And I couldn't help thinking Dad was trying to convince himself he didn't love hosting *Passport to Paranormal* as much as I knew he did. He'd told me he hadn't made his decision yet, but it seemed pretty obvious to me that he had. He wanted to take the talk show job and move back to Ohio.

It wasn't what he *wanted*, it's what he thought was *best*. For me.

Maybe the thing that bothered me most of all was that a small part of me wondered if he was right. I'd agreed to go to my mother's bridal shower in March, which was a huge step ... but our relationship was still pretty damaged. And I was being haunted by a ghost version of myself. I'd thought a lot about why the Thing would shred Dad's contract, and I suspected it was because it *did* want to go back to Ohio. After all, it was the me my mom wanted. I imagined pretty ghost-me floating down the aisle in my bridesmaid dress at my mother's wedding and snickered, which I quickly disguised as a snore.

Whether the Thing was actually real or not, I had some serious issues.

After nearly two hours, the van slowed to a halt. I hung the Elapse around my neck and grabbed my backpack before hopping out. The cold air definitely had a bite to it, but it wasn't nearly as frigid as New York had been. Just down the dirt road, I spotted an entrance to the bridge. Oscar slid out of the van and joined me.

"Wow."

"Yeah." The sun was just beginning to set between the mountains, and between that and the low clouds and fog, the sky was a beautiful haze of deep blues, purples, and pinks. As my eyes adjusted to the dim light, I could see bits and pieces of the bridge clinging to the sides of the mountains and disappearing in the distance, like it went on forever. Well, that explained why it was called the "Eternity" bridge. My fingers itched for my camera, but I resisted the urge to start taking photos. I didn't need the Elapse's weird anxiety aura kicking in any earlier than necessary.

Oscar glanced over at the crew unloading equipment from the back of the van. "So, gonna give the thoughtography thing another try?"

I frowned. "I don't know. I guess I could try." In truth, I was still so distracted by the conversation with my dad that I wasn't sure I could focus enough.

"I think Jamie's right," Oscar said. "It might not get rid of the Thing, but it's a good first step to figure out how."

I smiled a little. "Unless I'm crazy, and there is no ghost."

Oscar looked at me sharply. "What?"

"What?" I shrugged. "Come on. You know that's a possibility. It's like when I first told you about Sonja. You believed I *thought* I'd seen her, but—"

"Kat, I believe you," Oscar said firmly. "I believe it's real. I promise."

My throat tightened a little. "Thanks. But just because I believe it's real doesn't mean it is."

I regretted bringing this up at all, because Oscar was starting to look genuinely concerned. "Why are you saying this all of a sudden?"

"It's not all of a sudden." I tried to keep my tone light. "Just, you know, crazy people don't usually know they're crazy, right? Emily probably didn't." I cringed. "Sorry."

He waved dismissively. "Whatever. Look, Kat. You're not crazy. I'm not just saying that to be supportive—you're *not*. Neither was Emily."

I gaped at him. "What? Of course she was."

"She's obsessive," Oscar said. "And she's dangerous. And she's in a psychiatric hospital, so maybe she had . . . I don't know, maybe she was sick, too. But . . ." He glanced over at the crew again and lowered his voice. "Look, a lot of people have called Aunt Lidia crazy. Between her seizures and her obsession with ghosts . . . when Levi died when they were teenagers, Aunt Lidia was *positive* his ghost was still following her around. Her friends called her crazy—even my grandmother did. But she wasn't. And . . . and even if she *had* been wrong about Levi, if it was just that she'd been—I don't know, traumatized by his death—that wouldn't make her *crazy*, either. It's not a nice thing to call someone. Including yourself."

I stared at Oscar. His gaze had drifted off to the sunset, and I had the distinct impression this wasn't just about Lidia or me. "You're right," I said softly. "I'm sorry."

He lifted a shoulder, and I could see his face tense, like he was worried I'd say something else. And I wanted to. I wanted to tell him that his obsession with what had happened with Emily, the fact that he couldn't let go of it, that it was making him paranoid—that didn't make him crazy, either. But he clearly didn't want to hear it, so I stayed silent.

"Kat! Oscar!" Lidia waved at us, and I saw Jess and Mi Jin had their cameras out and ready. Oscar and I joined them, and Jess cleared her throat.

"Okay! I know it doesn't seem like it, but I've been told it's easy to get lost on this bridge. There are spots to get onto and off of hiking trails roughly every three kilometers. This fog's only going to get thicker—we probably won't even be able to see the van from that entrance in a few hours. We're not going on any of the trails, so stick to the bridge, all right?"

Lidia handed out walkie-talkies as Jess talked. "These have a twenty-mile range, so we should be good. You two," she added to Oscar and me, "make sure you can see one of us at all times."

"We'll do the intro inside the entrance," Jess said, already walking. Oscar and I hung back as Dad launched into his explanation of the bridge, with Sam and Roland occasionally jumping in with additional observations (and, in Roland's case, snark). Jess filmed them speaking, while Mi Jin took video from farther back, framing all four of them against the misty mountain backdrop. Then, as a group, we headed out on the bridge.

It was wide enough for two people to walk comfortably side by side. Oscar walked next to the wall of grass and granite to our right, and I walked along the edge, trailing my fingers along the wooden railing. I could see what Jess meant about visibility; already, the entrance and our van had been swallowed by the fog behind us.

We slowed our pace gradually, until the adults were out of earshot. Then Oscar nudged me.

"Try it," he said, pointing to my camera.

I reached for it, then hesitated. "It's going to make us feel lost, though. Remember?"

"I know," Oscar replied. "But we can't actually *get* lost. All we have to do is just keep walking straight."

"True." I exhaled slowly, then flipped on the Elapse.

Immediately, my pulse quickened and I felt panic rising in my throat. Oscar crossed his arms tightly, his eyes darting around.

"Once we take care of your ghost, we really need to do something about your camera," he said, and I laughed nervously.

"Yeah. It's annoying." *Annoying* wasn't really a strong enough word for the anxiety coursing through me. "It wasn't this bad at the Montgomery, was it?"

Oscar shook his head. "Nope."

"I wonder why."

"More people?" he suggested. "Jamie and Hailey were in the elevator, plus the operator. Maybe the more people there are to . . . to absorb the negative energy or whatever it is, the weaker it feels."

I tried to laugh, but it came out shaky. "If that's the case, remind me never to use this camera alone."

He smiled. "So . . . gonna try it?"

Nodding, I wiped one hand on my jeans, then the other. There was a curve up ahead, and I could hear Roland's voice just on the other side. "Stop," I said, grabbing Oscar's elbow. My heart was pounding so hard it felt like it was trying to break out of my rib cage. "Look out there, those two cliffs— do you see that?"

Oscar squinted at where I was pointing. The light was growing dimmer by the minute, and the sky was rapidly darkening from ocean blue to black. From where we stood, different parts of the bridge were visible through the clouds. And one part—a very short part—connected the narrow gap between two staggeringly tall, spindly rocks. The drop below into the mist was dizzying.

"Yeah," Oscar breathed. "Wow."

I could still hear Roland and Sam talking, punctuated by Dad's laughter. "They stopped, too." I fumbled with the Elapse, my fingers shaking with completely unnecessary nerves. "Let me know when they start moving again."

I held the viewfinder to my eye, zoomed in on the space between the two rocks, and found the bridge. While the walking path it offered was straight, the gray stones that supported it beneath arched gracefully from one side to the other. The railings were about waist-high, and I was pretty sure they were also made from stone—carved into a cool, abstract pattern, but sturdy-looking nonetheless. The rocks rose up several feet higher than the bridge itself; there must have been tunnels cut through both, but they weren't visible from this angle. The overall impression was that a tiny bridge had been sandwiched between two giant cliffs.

I imagined the Thing standing on it. Clutching that railing, long hair fluttering in the breeze, staring right back at me. I imagined it trapped there. Forever. Watching me as I got in the van and drove away and never came back.

"Kat." Oscar squeezed my arm, his voice high and weird. I gasped, pressing the shutter button. *Click.*

"What, did you see it?" I lowered my camera quickly. Then I realized Oscar was looking at me, not the bridge.

"No, you weren't responding. I said your name like five times. The others are walking; we have to follow them."

He was standing right next to me, but his voice sounded weirdly far away. I felt strange . . . like I'd just done a roller-coaster loop, upside down and around and back to where I started in a matter of seconds, but with my insides all swoopy and scrambled.

Oscar reached out and turned off the Elapse. Then he tugged me forward. "Hurry, before they get too far ahead."

We walked quickly, and when we rounded the curve, I saw the cast huddled up not far from the section of the bridge I'd just been photographing. They were deep in discussion, staring into the tunnel I now saw cut through the first rock.

"Better, right?" Oscar said, and it took me a second to realize he meant the lost feeling.

"Oh. Yeah."

The anxiety that came with using the Elapse was gone. But I still felt weird.

Oscar and I continued up the bridge, which inclined quite a bit, and stopped quietly a few feet from the rest of the crew. This was only a few feet higher, but the distance was startling; thick fog swirled around us, and white clouds hung so low I thought maybe I could graze them with my fingers if I got a running jump. Dad walked through the tunnel and out onto that small, high segment of bridge between the two rocks, Mi Jin right behind him. He was calling out, but I couldn't hear what he was saying.

"I'd love to know how they got ahead of us," Roland said mildly. Next to him, Lidia gripped her walkie-talkie, her mouth a thin line.

Jess swung her camera from the tunnel to Sam. "You didn't see them pass us when we stopped a few minutes ago?"

Roland snorted. "They aren't ghosts, so Sam didn't notice them."

"Who are you talking about?" Oscar asked, and the adults whirled around. I flinched at the sight of Jess's camera aimed right at me.

And Jess *screamed*.

CHAPTER SEVEN
KATYA THE NOT-SO-FRIENDLY GHOST

Monica Mills
Less than a month to the shower! All this planning is so
exhausting, I'll probably sleep through the wedding. ;)
Like • Comment • Share
Shonda Elfman, Christy Hopkins, and 21 others like this.

Kat Sinclair at 11:24am
Your real daughter will be home soon. And I'll never leave you
again.

I'd heard Jess yell before. Shout. Gasp. Shriek with laughter,
even.

But I'd never, *never* heard her scream like this.

Oscar and I gaped at her, too stunned to speak. Roland
snatched her camera before it hit the ground. Jess tore her
eyes off me as she grabbed it, and held it back up. "How'd
you do that?" she demanded. Sam watched me closely, his
mouth slightly open, and Lidia's eyes were huge behind her
glasses. Even Roland seemed a little rattled. Dad and Mi Jin
came running out of the tunnel, coming to an abrupt halt
when they saw me.

Six pairs of eyes and two cameras, all pointed at me.

My skin went clammy and cold.

"What?" Oscar said, looking from them to me and back again. "Why's everyone freaking out?"

"Have you two been behind us this whole time?" Roland asked.

"Yeah, obviously," Oscar replied. "Like you told us."

"We saw Kat," Jess said firmly. "Over there, through that tunnel."

"We *thought* we saw a girl," Roland corrected her. "And you and Jack thought it was Kat."

"I'm telling you, I zoomed in on her face," Jess argued. "It *was* Kat."

I struggled to keep my shock from showing. Had they actually seen the Thing?

Dad walked over to me, eyes filled with concern. "You're okay?"

"Of course," I said, though my heart was racing again. "Oscar and I stopped back there for a minute and I took some pictures. Then we followed you guys over here. That's it, I swear."

Dad put his arm around my shoulders and turned back to Jess and her camera. "I thought I saw her, too, Jess," he said. "But there's no one on that part of the bridge, and Kat's obviously right here, so . . ."

"I zoomed *in*," Jess repeated, her eyes flashing. All traces of fear were gone; now she looked excited. "It was her face. Look, I'll show you the playback—"

"No, keep it rolling," Roland interrupted. "I think you're all missing the point. We all saw *something*, right? Something potentially paranormal? And we're supposed to be paranormal investigators, so hey. Let's maybe investigate."

Snickering, Mi Jin followed him back to the tunnel. Jess and Lidia exchanged bemused looks, then headed after them. So did Sam, after giving me one last curious glance. Dad squeezed my shoulders.

"You believe me, right?" I asked him.

"Yes," he said immediately, and I breathed a sigh of relief. "I really thought I saw you out there, though. It was the weirdest thing. I can't wait to see what Jess got on camera."

Me either, Oscar mouthed at me, and I managed a small smile. But my heart was pounding again, even harder now than it had been when the cameras were on me. *Proof. Proof. Proof.*

The three of us started walking toward the tunnel, and when I was sure Dad wasn't watching, I flipped on the Elapse. I just needed to see that picture I took of the bridge. Had I really projected the Thing? And not just into my camera, but in real life?

But instead of a picture, the screen flashed a message.

Low battery

And then it powered itself off.

Dad glanced at me. "You okay?"

"Yeah," I said lightly, tapping the Elapse to hide the fact

that my fingers were shaking. "Battery's dead."

He frowned. "Already? Did you forget to charge it?"

"I guess so."

Another lie. When I turned the Elapse on five minutes ago, it had been fully charged. Then, one photo later, it was dead.

It looked like my attempt at psychic photography hadn't been a failure, after all.

It was quarter to midnight by the time we got back to the hotel. We'd gotten plenty of creepy footage: the mist creeping up the bridge and over our feet like spindly fingers, rocky cliffs disappearing into the clouds, words in Mandarin scratched into the stone railings. Sam and Lidia had spent a full thirty minutes in one spot, both claiming to feel a gentle pushing sensation on their backs.

But when we gathered in Jess's hotel room to review the video, it was obvious the only thing everyone really wanted to see was the thing on the bridge. And Oscar and I wanted to see if it was *the* Thing.

We'd huddled together in the backseat of the van on the drive back, talking about what had happened in hushed tones. I'd noticed Dad glancing at me in the rearview mirror a few times, and I couldn't help feeling guilty. I hadn't lied to him, but I definitely wasn't telling him the full story. I was still too afraid of what his reaction would be if he knew.

Now, I watched as Mi Jin tried to hook up Jess's camera

to the TV. "It's not gonna work," she said, tossing a few cords on the floor. "We don't have the right adapter."

"Laptop will do," Jess replied. "Hand me the cable." Her eyes sparkled as she connected her camera to the laptop, and I glanced around at everyone else. No one was saying it, but I could see the anticipation on their faces. My breathing grew shallow, and I closed my eyes, trying to relax. I'd been so preoccupied wondering about the Thing, I hadn't really considered how potentially huge this could be for the show. Actual footage of a ghostly figure.

Dad's face filled the laptop screen, and Jess pressed fast forward. "Hope no one minds if I skip ahead," she said.

Roland thumped his fist on the desk three times. "Let's see some ghost Kat!" he joked, and everyone laughed. I smiled, but my lungs felt squeezed tight.

"Here we go." Jess sat back, and the room fell silent.

The laptop's volume was too low for me to hear from where I was sitting, but it didn't matter. I watched the screen as Roland talked into the camera. Just behind him, Dad was looking around, hand in his pockets. Then his eyes widened, and he pointed. The camera swung in that direction, and there was the tunnel entrance. I could see the mist swirling around the bridge on the other side. And in that mist, very distinctly, was a figure. It was too foggy to make out much detail, but it was there, standing by the railing, the profile of its face barely visible.

But very familiar.

I held my breath. The next part happened quickly. Dad headed for the tunnel, calling my name. The camera zoomed in. The fog churned in a particularly strong breeze. The figure turned and faced the tunnel, and I felt a jolt of recognition—my eyes, my nose, my mouth. Then there was the distant sound of Oscar's voice, the camera whipped around, and there was the real me. On-screen Jess's scream came loud and clear through the laptop's speakers, and the camera fell.

Jess pressed pause, and the screen froze. For a second, no one spoke. Then Roland swore softly under his breath.

"Play it again," Dad said. His voice was weirdly flat. Jess didn't reply, just hit rewind. This time, she played it back in slow motion. And when the figure on the bridge turned to face the camera, she hit pause.

It was the Thing. No question. Most of its body was shrouded in mist, but I was pretty sure it was wearing a dress, and I'd bet anything it had a long braid down its back.

Jess hit play again, and the slow motion resumed. The footage moved slowly, seamlessly, as the camera swung around from me on the other side of the tunnel to me on the bridge behind Jess.

No editing. No tricks. A ghost Kat, and then the real Kat.

Passport to Paranormal had never captured anything like this footage before.

Once again, everyone turned to look at me. My face burned, and I shook my head, unwilling to speak. I needed to be alone, I had to think about this. What did it mean?

Mi Jin broke the silence. "A doppelganger," she said excitedly, clasping her hands on top of her head. "It's a flipping *doppelganger*. I've researched them a ton for my screenplay. Wow. *Wow*."

Then everyone started talking at once, and they all had different theories. Astral projection. A reflection in the fog. An illusion caused by the demonic spirit that guarded the bridge. Jess rewound and played the video for a third time, then a fourth. Only Oscar and I stayed silent. Because we didn't have to theorize. We already knew what it was.

And here was the proof I needed to show Dad I wasn't losing my mind. Or was it? What would Dad say if I told him that the ghost Jess had captured had ripped up his contract? Maybe he'd think I was just using it as a convenient excuse. Or maybe he'd believe me. Could I take that risk, when the consequence might be leaving the show for good?

"Kat. Are you okay?" Dad was suddenly at my side, and I blinked.

"Yeah." I stood up abruptly. "I'm fine. Just . . . tired."

"Oh, Kat. I'm sorry." Jess closed her laptop. "I didn't mean to frighten you."

"No, I'm not scared," I said, but my shaky voice gave me away. "It's just kind of freaky, that's all."

Mi Jin looked closely at me. "Have you seen it before?"

"No!" I avoided Oscar's gaze and willed him not to say anything. I didn't know what to say. I just needed time to

82

think. *Alone.* "No, never. I need to . . . can I go to bed? Sorry, I just—"

"Of course," Dad said immediately. "I'll walk with you."

"It's right down the hall," I protested feebly, but Dad was already steering me toward the door. Neither of us spoke until we were back in my room. Dad closed the door and turned to face me.

"Are you okay, Kat?" His brows were knit with worry.

I swallowed, nodding. "Fine."

"Do you want me to stay?" he asked, and I shook my head.

"I'm not scared." It came out way too defiant.

He sighed. "Okay. I'll be right down the hall if you need me." Dad put his hand on the doorknob, then paused. "Kat, sweetie . . . is there anything else you want to tell me?"

"No," I whispered. "I'm just tired, that's all."

"Okay." Dad smiled at me. But as he turned to go, I caught another expression on his face.

He looked defeated.

The door clicked closed softly, and I headed for the desk. The moment I plugged the Elapse in to charge, my phone buzzed in my pocket. I pulled it out to find a text from Oscar.

OB: This is crazy.

I laughed shakily.

KS: You said not to use that word.

OB: I meant about people.

This was followed by an eyeroll emoji.

KS: Do you think they believed I never saw it before?
OB: Think so. Mi Jin's really into this doppelganger idea.

I took a deep breath.

KS: Good. If they think they have an explanation, maybe they won't ask me for one.
OB: I know you don't want to tell them about the Thing, but what about thoughtography? They know you went to that exhibit, it makes sense that you wanted to try it. And it won't make the footage any less cool.
KS: But it wasn't thoughtography.
OB: What? But you projected it! Right?

I pictured the two staircase photos again. One with a ghost, one without. Because the first photographer had projected it.

KS: If it was a psychic photo, it'd only show up on my camera. But Jess got it, too. And besides, THEY ALL SAW IT. With their actual eyes. That's not thoughtography.
OB: Ok . . . so what does that mean?
KS: It means I didn't project the Thing. It chose to be there.

Exhaling slowly, I sat on the edge of my bed before adding:

KS: So I can't control it.

CHAPTER EIGHT
STAY TUNED FOR
DOOM

P2P Wiki
Entry: "Doppelgangers"
Edited by: Maytrix

An apparition of a living person, also called a "double."
Traditionally, if a person sees their doppelganger, it's thought to
mean bad luck. In some cultures, doppelgangers are believed to
be harbingers of death. Others think a doppelganger serves as
an "evil twin," or another version of that person but with dark
intentions.

AFTER a rushed breakfast the next morning, Dad and Jess headed out for a full schedule of back-to-back interviews with locals, all of whom had different stories about their experiences on the Yongheng Bridge. Lidia was busy taking care of logistics for our episode in Seoul next week, and Roland and Sam started editing the footage from the bridge.

Oscar and I had just finished plates of scrambled eggs and soft steamed buns filled with pork when Mi Jin slid into the chair next to me. I saw her camera in her lap and groaned.

"I don't wanna."

Mi Jin smiled sympathetically. "Well, you gotta. We can't

have an episode where an actual apparition of one of our own cast members appears, and then not interview that cast member about it." I made a face, and she added: "Or we could get started on Algebra II. Spring semester has begun, my lovely students."

Oscar was already getting to his feet. "Interview, Kat," he pleaded. "Is being on camera really worse than homework?"

"Is eating a tarantula really worse than drinking snake venom?" I muttered, but I stood, too. When I woke up this morning, Dad had warned me about this interview, so Oscar and I had spent the last half hour planning out how I'd respond—because clearly I wasn't going to talk about the Thing and my issues with my mother on national television. I knew what I had to say. I just had to make it convincing.

We found a quiet corner of the lobby, where a large painting featured misty mountains similar to the ones we'd visited yesterday. The picture was in black and white, except for the moon, which was bloodred.

"Perfect backdrop," Mi Jin said, positioning me in front of it. Oscar stepped forward hesitantly.

"Both of us, or just Kat?"

Mi Jin chewed her lip for a moment. Then she thrust her camera at Oscar.

"Me and Kat."

Oscar blinked. "What?"

"I want you to film me and Kat," Mi Jin said, helping him hoist the camera onto his shoulder. "I know a lot about doppelgangers, and it makes more sense for me to be on camera talking to her about it. Do you mind?"

"No!" Actually, Oscar looked pleased. He listened carefully as Mi Jin showed him the various buttons. Then she hurried over to join me.

"Ready." She laughed when I made a gagging face. "I know this isn't your favorite part, but you're always great on camera. All right, Oscar—go for it!"

The red light flashed on, and Mi Jin turned to me.

"So, Kat. After watching that footage of you and the ghost on the bridge about a zillion times, the whole crew agrees that there's no way it's some sort of reflection. We saw an apparition, and it looked exactly like you. Everyone has different theories, but what do you think it was?"

I took a deep breath. "I think you're right. I think it's a doppelganger."

Mi Jin's eyebrows shot up. "Really? Why?"

"Well, Sam mentioned astral projection," I began. "I researched that, and usually the person is unconscious or meditating and they project their—their soul, or spirit or whatever—to another location, and then they see what their spirit sees. Obviously, I was conscious the whole time, and I didn't have any sort of out-of-body experience." The memory of that roller-coaster loop sensation hit me, and I pushed it away. "Then Lidia and Jess thought maybe it was the demonic presence that supposedly haunts the bridge, and . . . well, I guess we'll see what my dad finds out during his interviews today, but I know he did a lot of research before we came and I don't remember any accounts of people saying they saw *themselves* on the bridge. A doppelganger is the only thing that makes sense."

Mi Jin did a little fist pump. "*Yes.* Exactly." She winked at the camera and added, "I'm a little bit obsessed with doppelgangers, so I'm really excited about this."

"I researched those, too," I went on, itching to get this over with. "They're supposed to be bad luck, if you see your own. Some people think it means you're going to die soon."

"True, but I have a theory about that," Mi Jin said. "Do you know what a self-fulfilling prophecy is?"

"Yes," I replied instantly. "It happens in books all the time. Someone hears a prophecy, and then when they try to do something to stop it, their actions just cause the prophecy to come true. So it's like it never would've happened if they hadn't heard the prophecy to begin with."

Mi Jin smiled. "Exactly! A lot of the recorded accounts I've read of people who have died after supposedly seeing their doppelgangers . . . their deaths were a result of their reaction to seeing it. You know what I mean? Like, if they hadn't freaked out after seeing their double, they wouldn't have gotten on that train that crashed or whatever led to their death."

"Yeah, that makes sense." I frowned. "Although . . . you're still basically saying if they hadn't seen their doppelganger, they wouldn't have died. So it *is* a . . ." I paused, trying to remember what I'd read on the *P2P* Wiki. "A *harbinger of death*."

Mi Jin looked impressed. "Touché. I guess it can be, depending on how the person reacts."

Out of the corner of my eye, I saw Oscar wave at me, and I knew what he wanted me to say. While we were brainstorming, he'd come up with the perfect way to end this interview. Bracing myself, I tore my eyes off Mi Jin, faced the camera, and smiled.

"Will I die in the season two finale? Tune in to find out!"

I held the smile another second, praying it looked natural. Then, mercifully, the red light turned off. Oscar struggled to lower the camera, but he was beaming.

"That was *awesome*," he said fervently. Feeling rather proud, I turned to Mi Jin. She wasn't smiling, though. In fact, she looked kind of shocked.

"Kat, you don't . . . are you actually worried you're going to die?"

"What? No!" I exclaimed. "Not at all. Oscar and I just thought that would be funny."

"And it's a great sound bite for finale promo," Oscar added. "Isn't it?"

Mi Jin relaxed a little. "Yeah, it would be . . ." She gave me an uncertain look. "Not sure your dad would be on board with that, though. I mean, promoting an episode based on whether or not you'll *die*?"

I wrinkled my nose. "I guess he probably won't like that."

Oscar's shoulders sagged. "So should we shoot something else?" he asked, and I groaned loudly.

Laughing, Mi Jin took her camera from him. "No, no . . . we'll see what he says. But even if he doesn't like that part, Kat, this interview was *great*. Love how you debunked those other theories."

"Thanks!"

"All right, off to do some editing." Mi Jin waved before heading to the elevators. Once she was out of sight, Oscar turned to me.

"You," he said, holding up his hand, "should consider being an actor, too."

I rolled my eyes. "Over my dead body," I replied, but I high-fived him, anyway.

Oscar and I spent most of the afternoon exploring the neighborhood, taking pictures of the giant colorful gate a few blocks away and ducking into a coffee and tea shop when the wind got too chilly. When we got back to the hotel, Oscar headed for the business center, a small room near the reception desk with several computers.

"Can't you use one of the laptops upstairs?" I asked, stifling a yawn.

He shook his head. "They're all up there editing, remember?"

"Ah." I glanced at the time on my phone. "They'll be stopping for dinner soon, though. Or, hey, you can always use the one in my room!"

"Yeah, but . . ." Oscar glanced at me and sighed. "I'm supposed to video chat with Thiago in fifteen minutes, okay?"

I grinned. "Ah." Thiago was a boy we'd met in Buenos Aires, and he and Oscar had really hit it off. "In that case, I think I'm gonna just go upstairs and take a nap. Tell Thiago I said hi."

When I stepped off the elevator, I remembered I needed to let Lidia know that Oscar and I were back. Her door was slightly ajar, but I knocked anyway before stepping inside. The usual mess greeted me: cables and cords all over the floor, five open laptops on the desk and beds, Lidia's giant whiteboard covered in notes blocking most of the window. Lidia was standing behind Roland, who was seated at the desk watching a clip.

"Hey, Lidia," I called, and she glanced up. "Oscar's downstairs in the business center, and I'm going to take a nap." Lidia gave me a thumbs-up and returned her attention to the screen. I barely had one foot back in the hall when Mi Jin yelled, "Kat, wait up!"

She joined me in the hall a moment later and thrust a thick stack of papers into my hands. I let out an exaggerated groan.

"Aw, is this homework?"

"Ha, no." Mi Jin stuck her hands in her pockets. "It's my screenplay. Doesn't have a title yet," she added, and I saw that the top page just said *UNTITLED, by Mi Jin Seong*.

"Oh, cool!" I said, suddenly feeling much more awake. "About doppelgangers, right? You're letting me read it?"

"Actually, I was hoping you'd give me some feedback."

My eyes widened. "What?"

"It's just a first draft," she said quickly. "I know it needs a lot of work. But it's basically about a woman who's being stalked by what she thinks is her doppelganger, and I just thought, hey, now I actually *know* someone who's seen her own doppelganger, plus she's a horror movie expert and a generally awesome human, so maybe she could give me some notes?"

Mi Jin clasped her hands together like she was begging, her eyes comically wide. I just stood there, floored. Mi Jin was one of the coolest and smartest people I'd ever met, and she was asking *me* for help? The idea made me feel extremely proud and terribly anxious at the same time.

"You . . . I . . . what . . ." I sputtered, then blushed. "But you're *my* teacher. How can I give you notes?"

"Um, besides all the reasons I just said?" Mi Jin said with a little laugh. "Hey, if it helps, think of this as a critical reading assignment. If you want to read it, of course."

"I do!" I said quickly. "I want to! I just . . . I don't know if I'll be much help."

"I know you will," Mi Jin said, beaming. "Thanks!" She gave me a quick hug, then headed back inside Lidia's room. I walked slowly down the hall to my room, hugging the screenplay to my chest and feeling all warm inside.

I was just sliding my key card through the lock when I heard the *ping* of the elevator on the other end of the hall. I glanced over to see Dad and Jess stepping off.

"Hey!" I said, pushing the door open but waiting in the hall. "Done with the interviews?"

"Yup!" Jess said cheerfully. "Got some great stuff." She headed into Lidia's room, but Dad said, "I'll be right there," and continued down the hall toward me. At the sight of his expression, my good mood vanished.

"Is something wrong?"

Dad didn't answer, just gestured for me to enter our room. Once we were inside, he exhaled slowly, then pulled out his phone.

"Your mother e-mailed me," he said. "She's pretty upset about this." He held his phone out, and I saw some Facebook status update my mom had written about her wedding. Then I noticed the first comment below it. A comment from me.

Your real daughter will be home soon. And I'll never leave you again.

My jaw dropped. "I didn't write that."

Dad tilted his head. "Do you think your account was hacked?" He said it like he was ready to believe me if I said yes, which made me feel even worse. Because it *had* been hacked, of course. But by the Thing, so once again, I couldn't tell the complete truth.

"It must have been, yeah," I croaked. "Or something. Because I didn't say that. I would *never* say that."

"It's just that . . ." Dad glanced at the screen and sighed. "Okay, I'll be honest. Your mother and I are both concerned that this is your way of trying to tell us something that you're too afraid to just . . . *say.*"

I blinked, then blinked again. "What?"

"Your real *daughter,"* Dad read aloud, and I flinched. "Does this mean . . . as opposed to Elena?"

"What?" My mind was so full of the Thing, it took me a minute to register what Dad was implying. "Dad, I don't care that Mom's about to have a stepdaughter. I *don't.*"

Another lie. Mom doted on Elena like she never had with me, and yes, it bugged me. But I'd never say anything so rude about her; especially not online, where my whole family could see it.

Maybe that showed on my face, because Dad looked disappointed. "And then this part, about never leaving again." He lowered his phone, and the sadness in his eyes made my throat clench up. "Between this and my contract, I just . . . Kat, do you want to go back to Chelsea for good? To be closer to your mom? Because, sweetie, *that's okay.* It won't hurt my feelings if that's what you want."

And he really didn't look hurt. He just looked so *sad.* The idea that he thought I'd rather be with Mom than with him hit me so hard, I couldn't even get out a *no.* I just burst into tears, burying my face in my hands. Dad immediately wrapped his arms around me, which just made me cry harder. After several minutes of sobbing (and eventually, hiccuping) into his sweater, I pulled away and wiped my nose.

"I *don't*," I said as firmly as I could, but my voice wobbled and cracked. "I swear, I don't. I want to be here with you." I walked over to my bed and lay down face-first, unable to look him in the eyes anymore. Exhaustion settled over me like a heavy blanket. Dad was silent for a few seconds.

"Kat?"

"I'm tired," I croaked into my pillow. "Can we talk about this later?"

Another pause. "Okay. I'll be down the hall if you need me."

A few seconds later, I heard the door click closed. I rolled over on my back and stared at the ceiling.

Your real daughter. When I'd first read that, before Dad mentioned Elena, I'd felt like I was on the brink of a realization. I lay still, hoping my brain would finish making the connection. *Your real daughter . . .* I closed my eyes and saw Laurie in the lobby of the Montgomery, asking for my autograph.

"What did you mean about meeting the real you?"

I sat up in bed, then lunged for my laptop. The Real Kat Sinclair—someone had left a few comments under that name on a *Rumorz* post and in the forums. It didn't take me long to find them. The first was on Shelly Mather's poll about the guest star. *You won't care about any of these idiots once you meet me.* And the second was on the forum thread when I'd "confirmed" that my dad was staying on the show next season. *I can't wait to leave this stupid show and go home for good.*

I wiped my eyes furiously. Now I knew what the Thing was doing. It was making sure I moved back to Ohio permanently. And it was doing a killer job of it, too. Judging by the heartbroken look on Dad's face, I wouldn't be surprised if he wasn't telling Jess and the others right now that the next episode would be his last.

Slamming the laptop closed, I sat there and fumed for nearly a minute. The only way to stop the Thing would be to tell Dad *about* the Thing. Except that wouldn't work at all, because whether Dad believed me or not—whether he thought I was being tormented by a ghost or just "crazy"— he'd definitely want to leave the show. And if I *didn't* tell him about the Thing, he'd just go on believing I was doing and saying all this horrible stuff because I was afraid to tell him I really wanted to be with Mom. Solution: again, Ohio.

No matter what I did, the Thing would win.

I was moving back to Chelsea.

CHAPTER NINE
THE GIRL WHO CRIED DOPPELGANGER

INTERIOR: ATTIC—NIGHT

LEE climbs the ladder into her grandmother's attic. She pulls a chain and the single overhead bulb flickers on, casting dim light onto dusty boxes, trunks, and old furniture. Lee looks around somberly. She wanders over to a box and opens it. A flurry of dust makes her cough.

> **LEE (amused)**
> So you weren't a total clean freak then, Gran?

She turns around and gasps at the sight of her own reflection. Then she laughs when she realizes it's just a tarnished old mirror. As she steps away, we see in the reflection a dark figure moving swiftly but silently in the shadows. Lee moves toward an old dresser against the wall.

> **LEE (softly)**
> What the . . .

Lee picks up a small figurine. It's identical to the princess figurine on her dresser at home, but this one is blackened, as if it has been burned. Clearly puzzled, Lee turns around, still gazing at the figurine, and finds herself face to face with her doppelganger. It's identical to her except for its eyes, which are solid black. Lee drops the figurine and screams at the top of her lungs, stumbling back against the dresser and knocking off the mirror. It shatters on the floor, and Lee runs to the ladder and hurriedly climbs down. The doppelganger picks up a shard of mirror and studies its reflection for a moment. Then, gripping the shard like a knife, it slowly follows after Lee.

THE business center was deserted, and I yawned hugely as I pulled out the rolling chair in front of the nearest computer. It was five to eight in the morning, which was absurdly early for me, but the twelve-hour time difference between Beijing and Ohio made it necessary. After plugging in my headphones, I signed into my e-mail and made sure the *available* option was checked in my video chat window.

Once Dad had gone to bed, I'd huddled under the covers and read Mi Jin's screenplay by the light of my phone. Weirdly, reading a story about someone's horrifying struggle with their evil doppelganger was the perfect distraction from my actual real-life experience with one.

I hadn't made any notes, though. Not yet. I was nervous about that part. Mi Jin had asked for feedback, and I was torn between fear of criticizing her work and offending her, and fear of *not* criticizing her work and letting her down.

I did have some ideas of how to make it better, though. Overall, it was an awesome story, and I could totally picture it in my head as a movie. But as I'd read, I'd found myself mentally rewriting some parts, changing a little bit here and there. Which, I knew, was what Mi Jin wanted me to do. It was just that actually telling her what to do with her screenplay seemed really . . . arrogant.

A soft *boop-beep* interrupted my thoughts.

trishhhhbequiet is calling you. Accept?

I clicked *Yes*, and a moment later, Trish and Mark appeared on the screen. The sight of the two of them in Trish's room, where the three of us had spent so much time together in sixth and seventh grade, gave me the strangest feeling every time we video chatted. It was equal parts happiness, wistfulness, and a third emotion I never let myself think about too hard.

"Hey!" Trish exclaimed, adjusting her laptop screen. "Whoa, you look tired."

"Thanks," I said dryly. "It's eight in the *morning* for me, you know. Hi, Fang!"

Grinning, Trish glanced over her shoulder at the tank on her dresser, where her pet snake was coiled up. "He says hi."

"What was the bridge like?" Mark pushed his glasses up his nose and leaned forward eagerly. "We already read your blog post. See anything creepy?"

I hesitated. I hadn't told Trish and Mark about the Thing, because . . . well, for a lot of reasons. Mostly because I knew how ridiculous it would sound to anyone who lived in the suburbs and went to school like normal kids, instead of spending every hour of every day with a bunch of ghost hunters. But in a few days, the next episode of *P2P* would air. And everyone would see the Thing on television.

"Yeah," I said finally. "We did, actually."

I launched into a description of our trip out to the Yongheng Bridge. But I left out the part about me trying to project the Thing on my camera, about the weird, roller-coaster loop feeling it had left me with. And when I got to the part about the ghost having my face, I found myself telling them Mi Jin's doppelganger theory. As if this ghost version of myself had just appeared, and I had no idea why.

I was lying to my best friends. Just like I was lying to my dad. I didn't want to, not at all . . . but the longer I kept these secrets about the Thing, the more secrets there were to keep, the bigger the lie became. Like a cartoon snowball, rolling down a mountain and getting bigger and more out of control every second.

"And it's *on video*?" Trish said, her eyes huge. "Like we're actually going to see this thing during the episode?"

I tried not to flinch at *thing*. "Yeah. It's pretty wild."

Mark squinted at me. "Are you scared? I mean, that's pretty . . . I don't know. I'd be really freaked out."

"Eh, but she's not going back to the bridge," Trish said. "I doubt it's just going to show up in her hotel, you know? Like, it's not going to be just lying out by the pool or something."

I forced a laugh. "Especially considering it's forty degrees outside."

"Hang on . . ." Mark was tapping on his phone screen,

brow furrowed. "Maybe you haven't seen it, but what about this?" He held up his phone, and I saw he'd pulled up my last blog post. The one where I'd mentioned The Real Kat Sinclair commenter. "I figured it was just, you know, some random person using your name. But what if it's . . ."

"My doppelganger?" I grinned at him. "I thought you didn't believe in paranormal stuff, even after all the stories I've told you."

Mark's face reddened a bit. "I don't . . . mostly. But this is a weird coincidence. And we saw . . ."

He exchanged a glance with Trish, and my stomach tightened.

"You saw what?"

"We saw that comment you left on your mom's Facebook," Trish said, tugging at a few of her braids nervously. "It, um . . . well, it didn't sound like you."

I swallowed. "It *wasn't* me. Someone must've gotten into my account."

"Like your doppelganger?" Mark joked half-heartedly.

"Maybe. Or just . . . I don't know, trolls or something." I shrugged. "Anyway. What's new with—"

"What's the deal with your house?" Trish blurted it out, and I realized she'd probably been holding back that question since the moment our chat had started. "Is your dad gonna buy it?"

I took a deep breath. Here, at least, was something I could be perfectly honest about.

"I think so. And I think we might be moving back for good."

Trish let out a happy little squeal, then clamped her hands over her mouth. Mark blinked several times.

"Really? Why?"

So I told them the whole story: the job offer from *Live with Wendy*, Dad saying hosting *P2P* was too much work even though I *knew* he loved it, the way he was acting all moody, how he'd said he was mad at himself, *when my daughter's not being attacked by psychopaths in an abandoned prison, she's being harassed by trolls online and reporters in real life . . .* And finally, that he thought I'd shredded his *P2P* contract, that I'd left that comment on my mom's Facebook wall . . . that I actually *wanted* to move back to Chelsea.

When I finished, Trish and Mark both stayed silent for a few seconds. Finally, Mark cleared his throat and said:

"And you . . . you don't?"

"What, want to move back?" I asked, surprised. "No! I didn't say any of that stuff. It's not how I feel at *all*."

Trish was staring at a spot somewhere to the left of her laptop. "Obviously," she mumbled. It took me a moment to realize what I'd said.

"Sorry, I didn't mean . . ." I felt a blush creep up my neck. "Dad thinks I want to live closer to my mom, and I don't. That's all I meant."

"But otherwise, you'd be okay moving back here?" Mark asked tentatively.

I opened my mouth to say *of course*, because that's what you say when your best friends ask if you want to move back to be with them again, because that's what you actually *want*. Except that feeling was nagging at me again, the one I got every time we video chatted, every time I was reminded of the life I'd left behind in Chelsea. The feeling I ignored.

I was *glad*. I was glad I didn't live there anymore. I missed Trish and Mark and Grandma constantly, but come on—I was traveling all over the world, visiting haunted places with a TV show. I had new friends, I had a weirdly successful blog that was super fun to write . . . in just a few months, being a part of *Passport to Paranormal* had become . . . well, normal. The thought of losing all of this, of going back to the same old school, same old house, same old movie theater on weekends and no ghosts whatsoever . . .

It was kind of devastating, to be honest. But there was no way to tell my best friends that without hurting their feelings.

Unfortunately, my silence pretty much told them, anyway.

Trish smiled tightly. "I get it," she said. "Probably seems really boring around here compared to what you're doing." She sounded like she was genuinely trying to be understanding, which just made me feel worse.

"No it doesn't!" I said way too quickly. *Lie.* "I mean, this is . . . I miss you guys, I really do, and . . ." I sighed, closing my eyes and wishing I'd never brought up any of this. "I guess

I'm just upset Dad thinks I'd rather be with Mom than with him."

Mark frowned. "He doesn't think you want to *live* with her, right?"

Until this moment, the thought hadn't occurred to me. But then, very clearly, I imagined seeing that comment on my mom's wall from Dad's perspective. *Your real daughter will be home soon. And I'll never leave you again.*

"I don't know," I said, my voice breaking a little. "Maybe he does think that."

"Mark!" I heard Trish's mom calling from down the hall. "Your brother's parked outside!"

"Coming!" Mark called back.

"Nathan's driving now?" I asked, surprised.

Mark nodded. "Got his license right after New Year's. I'm surprised he passed the test . . . half the time he tries to park in front of the house, he runs up on the curb."

"And oh my God, last weekend," Trish said, her eyes brightening. "Kat, he took us to the mall, and he accidentally drove the wrong way down the little street that goes around the parking lot. He got pulled over."

"By a mall cop," Mark added. "In one of those little golf carts."

We all started giggling uncontrollably. "Trish, Mark!" Trish's mom yelled again. "It's almost nine o'clock!"

"All right!" Trish yelled back. She grinned at me, and I grinned back, relieved she didn't look all hurt and awkward anymore. "Maybe we can do this again when you get to . . . where exactly are you going next?"

"Seoul. And yes, definitely."

"Cool. Bye, Kat!"

I waved at them until the screen went black. Then I took off the headphones, logged out of my account, and rubbed my eyes. Breakfast sounded good, but bed sounded better.

I compromised by grabbing a napkin with as many steamed buns as I could carry and eating them on my way back up to my room. Talking to Trish and Mark had left me feeling unsettled. I hated lying to them, I hated that I'd hurt their feelings, I hated knowing that they would probably talk to each other about why I didn't want to move back to Chelsea, and say all the things they wouldn't say to my face . . .

And now I had something brand-new to worry about. Could Dad possibly think I wanted to live with Mom?

I entered my room and found the beds neatly made. Dad had gotten up when I did; I was pretty sure there was a conference call going on in Lidia's room. The cleaning staff must have come in right after we'd left. I kicked off my shoes and headed straight for my bed. But then I noticed my camera on the night table and froze.

I'd left the Elapse on top of Mi Jin's script, like a paperweight. But now, the script was gone.

For nearly ten minutes, I searched every place I could think of. The drawers, under the bed, on top of the TV. I even looked through Dad's paperwork on the desk, thinking maybe the cleaning staff had put all the papers together or something. Finally, I sat on the bed and stared at my reflection in the mirror. My stomach turned as I pictured my dad's contract, all torn to shreds.

The Thing had Mi Jin's script, I was positive. But what was it going to do to it?

CHAPTER TEN
PSYCHO(LOGY)

Rumorz
All the celebrity gossip you need (and then some)!
JACK SINCLAIR'S DAUGHTER SEES DEATH OMEN IN BEIJING
by Shelly Mathers

Spoilers ahead for episode 33 of *Passport to Paranormal*, which aired yesterday evening.

Last night's episode of *P2P* has stirred up a bit of controversy—almost as much as the infamous Daems Penitentiary episode, when the crew received an unwanted visit from former host Emily Rosinski! But this time, the visitor crashing the party wasn't human. Well, not quite.

A supposed "ghost" with a face bearing a remarkable resemblance to host Jack Sinclair's daughter, Kat, was spotted on the Yongheng Bridge . . . while Kat herself looked on from another part of the bridge. The startling footage sent the *P2P* fandom into overdrive; some have already posted their own reviews examining the clip frame by frame. Many seem to have latched on to the theory that the apparition was a doppelganger—including Kat Sinclair, who seemed unfazed by the incident and went so far as to tease the idea that the sighting may indicate she'll meet an untimely end in the season finale.

Her rather laid-back attitude has caused many fans to speculate that this is another of the show's infamous publicity stunts. Either way, one can't help but wonder what *P2P*'s latest host is thinking right now. Whether he's just using his daughter for ratings or putting her in real danger, Jack Sinclair isn't about to win Father of the Year.

AVOIDING someone is hard to do when you're traveling together. I spent our last few days in Beijing searching everywhere for Mi Jin's script—I even asked the receptionist to check with the cleaning staff to see if it had been accidentally thrown away—but it was gone. For now.

Obviously, Mi Jin had the script on her laptop, so it wasn't like the original was gone. But I was too embarrassed to admit to her that I'd lost the copy she'd given me. And I still hadn't figured out how to give her actual criticism. So I did the mature thing: total avoidance.

The night before we left for Seoul, the Yongheng Bridge episode aired. I pretended to have a stomachache and hid out in my room while everyone else watched it together. The next morning, I waited until she got into one airport van before hopping into the second. I hung in the back of the security line at the airport, then hid out at one of the shops in the concourse pretending to look at books while she and the rest of the crew got coffee. I walked five gates down to use the restroom just in case she decided to use the one closest to our gate.

"You're such a chicken," Oscar said when I slumped back down in the chair next to him. "Just tell her what happened and ask her for another copy."

"I don't need another copy," I muttered. "I already read it. She wants feedback from me."

"So tell her what you thought."

"But she wants me to, like, tell her things to *fix*."

"So tell her what to fix. You said you had some ideas."

"Oscar, it's not—I don't . . ." I sputtered. "It's *weird*. What do I know about writing?"

He shrugged. "Nothing, I guess. Except for the whole thing where you have a blog with like a billion followers."

"This is different," I argued, my face going hot. "It's a screenplay."

"Yeah. For a horror movie," Oscar agreed. "Like the kind your grandmother starred in. Like the kind you're totally obsessed with." He eyed the *Cannibal Clown Circus* tee I had on over my long-sleeved thermal shirt. "And base your entire wardrobe on."

I crossed my arms over the clown's grotesque smile. "Mi Jin's our *teacher*. And she's really smart, and . . ."

"And you're a chicken," Oscar finished, his expression smug. "Like I said."

I scowled, because I couldn't argue with that, because he was totally right. Someone cleared his throat, and the smile slipped from Oscar's face. I turned to see Roland settling into the chair behind mine, holding a giant coffee cup.

"Ready?" He directed the question at Oscar, who suddenly looked nervous.

"What's going on?" I asked.

"I asked Roland if I could talk to him about . . ." Oscar waved his hand vaguely. "You know. The Emily stuff."

"Oh!" I felt a rush of guilt. I'd been so wrapped up in my own problems lately, I'd completely forgotten about Oscar's. "Right. Um. I'll just . . ." I started to stand, but Oscar grabbed my arm.

"You can stay," he said quickly. "I mean, if you want."

"Yeah, okay."

Roland took a sip of his coffee. "So. The 'Emily stuff.'" He made air quotes, and Oscar sighed.

"Right."

For the next fifteen minutes, I sat quietly as Oscar told Roland all about how jumpy and paranoid he'd been lately, about how he kept replaying what had happened back at Daems in his mind like a waking nightmare.

I'd had vague unsettling dreams last night, like I did most nights now. The only detail I remembered was seeing words scratched into the bathroom mirror, just like the Thing had done back in Buenos Aires. Except it was slightly different. The words weren't *I got out*, but I couldn't quite recall what they were.

Also, in my dream, I was the one scratching them into the mirror.

"And I keep thinking I should've reacted faster," Oscar was saying. "I just . . . I saw her coming out of the cell, and I didn't react fast enough because I was so focused on Aunt Lidia. I should've . . . ducked. Or, I don't know, hit her." He rolled his eyes, as if even he found the thought of him physically fighting a stalker armed with a knife ridiculous. "Or . . . I could've at least warned Kat in time. I mean, Emily just dragged her off, she could've *killed* her, and it was my fault."

Surprised, I immediately opened my mouth to argue. But Roland touched my elbow, and I pressed my lips together. I hadn't realized Oscar had been feeling guilty about what Emily had done to me.

"I know you know this, Oscar," Roland said. "But everything Emily did was *Emily's* fault. Not yours, not anyone else's."

Oscar sighed. "Yeah, yeah. Aunt Lidia's said the same thing to me a million times. *You didn't do anything wrong.* Doesn't change the fact that I didn't do anything *right*, though. If I'd moved faster, Emily wouldn't have knocked me out. I could've run for help, or just . . . done *something*."

Roland raised his eyebrows. "I thought you said you hadn't talked to Lidia about this."

"I haven't."

"So her saying *you didn't do anything wrong* is about . . ."

"Oh." Oscar shot me a mildly panicked look. "Um. Something else."

An awkward silence fell. Roland took another sip of coffee. "Okay, well, you don't have to tell me," he said lightly. "But generally speaking, the more a patient discloses in therapy, the more he gets out of the session."

"It's just . . ." Oscar swallowed. "It's not relevant."

Roland grinned. "Ooh, I love when patients say that. They're always wrong."

I stifled a giggle, and Oscar shot me a dirty look. "Fine." He glanced around, then leaned forward and took a deep breath.

"Last year I told my best friend I had a crush on him and he freaked out and told everyone and they did a bunch of mean stuff and we got in a fight and I punched him and got expelled and yeah I *know* he's the bully not me and I *know* it's his fault not mine but that doesn't change the fact that if I hadn't said anything to begin with he wouldn't have bullied me and I wouldn't have punched him and I wouldn't have been expelled."

Oscar finally stopped, breathing heavily. He and I watched Roland carefully, but his expression hadn't changed.

"And when that happened, did you *replay* the situation?" he asked. "Like you're doing now, with Emily?"

"No."

"Oh, yes you did," I blurted out. "You kept the mean notes Mark wrote. To *read* them."

Oscar scowled. "Like you did with that troll's comments on your blog, you mean?"

"Okay," Roland cut in just as I opened my mouth. "One patient at a time." He rested his coffee cup on the armrest between Oscar's chair and mine. "Oscar, you said you know what happened in Brussels was Emily's fault. You said you know Mark's the bully. But I kinda think you don't fully believe that. Otherwise, you wouldn't be punishing yourself like this."

"Punishing myself?" Oscar repeated.

Roland nodded. "By imagining all the different things you could've done—or have *not* done. You know what Emily could've *not* done? Violently attacked a couple of kids. You know what your friend could've *not* done? Made your life miserable instead of being supportive, like a friend should." He drummed his fingers on the back of my chair, studying Oscar thoughtfully. "I'm wondering if this could be a pattern. Coping when someone mistreats you by blaming yourself."

Oscar shifted uncomfortably. "What? No, I—I just need to stop being all paranoid. I thought you could just, I don't know, give me antianxiety pills or something. So I can sleep."

"I can't prescribe anything until I have a diagnosis." Roland squinted at Oscar. "Antianxiety pills? Have you taken those before?"

I watched as Oscar became suddenly fixated on untying the knot on one of his hoodie's strings. "Yeah, a long time ago." Roland said nothing, just waited expectantly. After nearly half a minute, Oscar sighed. "When my dad went to prison."

"Ah." Roland leaned back, looking like someone who'd just found a missing puzzle piece. "I see."

I looked from Roland to Oscar and back again, my whole body tense. I'd talked to Oscar enough about his dad to know how this went. Push too hard, ask one too many questions, and he'd get all irritated and shut down.

But Roland didn't push or ask questions. He didn't

even look at Oscar. He just . . . sat there. Sipping his coffee, watching people walk past our gate, looking all calm and disinterested like he wasn't in the middle of an intense conversation.

So I followed his lead, gazing at the TV hanging under our gate number but watching Oscar out of the corner of my eye. He finished untying the knot, then tied it again, then double knotted it. Then, very quietly, he started talking again.

"I was in fifth grade during his trial. It was for embezzlement . . . I didn't even know what that meant. I still kind of don't. Anyway, since it was just me and my dad when I was little, he'd bring me to his café after school when he had to work late. I'd do my homework in his office, play games on his iPad . . . just hang out." Oscar paused, blinking several times. "He used to have meetings with this one guy after the café was closed. Mr. Boyle. He had this really ugly wig that he pretended wasn't a wig, it was kind of . . ." He shook his head. "Creepy-looking. Anyway. During the trial, my dad's lawyer told me the people trying to put my dad in prison were going to ask me questions, since I spent so much time with him at work. He told me to just be honest. So when I went up there, they asked if I'd ever seen Mr. Boyle before, and I said yes, and they asked where, and . . . and my dad was just sitting there, staring at me with this totally panicked look, it really freaked me out, right? But his lawyer had told me to be honest, so . . . so I told the truth.

114

That my dad and Mr. Boyle had some meetings after the café closed. And as soon as I said that, my dad just . . ." Oscar pressed his lips together, then looked up at Roland. "I could tell I'd messed up. I wasn't supposed to tell them about Mr. Boyle."

"It proved your dad was guilty?" I couldn't help asking.

Oscar nodded. "Basically. I mean, there was other evidence. But I guess once the other lawyers knew about those meetings with Mr. Boyle, they found a whole bunch of *other* evidence, and . . . yeah."

"You blamed yourself for your dad going to prison," I said in disbelief. "When you were in *fifth grade*? Oscar, that's . . ." I trailed off, because I'd almost said *crazy*. But I couldn't think of a better word. "You know it's not your fault."

"Yeah, well." Oscar shrugged. "Knowing it and believing it aren't the same thing."

Roland cleared his throat. "Sounds like we found the beginning of your pattern."

I gazed down at my hands, thinking hard. When I'd first met Roland, he'd said Oscar and I were a lot alike—and he'd been right. I'd punished myself by reading that troll's comments about me, just like Oscar had punished himself by reading Mark's notes. And even though I thought it was totally ridiculous that Oscar blamed himself for his father going to prison, I also understood why he felt that way.

After all, hadn't I always blamed myself for my mother leaving?

The first few times she'd bailed, I'd sworn to myself that if she came back, I'd be the perfect daughter. Well, her idea of a perfect daughter. Each time, my vow had only lasted a few weeks before I'd give up and just go back to being me. And each time, my vision of the Thing had grown stronger, clearer. The mother-approved version of myself I honestly believed could get her to stay. Then last spring, when Mom took off again, I hadn't been sad. I'd been *angry*. I thought I'd been angry at her. I mean, I *had* been angry at her.

But mostly, I'd been angry at myself.

I blamed myself for her leaving. I hated myself for it. I couldn't even stand seeing myself on camera, the ugly version of me that wasn't good enough, that drove Mom away.

It was just like Oscar said. I knew, logically, that my mother leaving wasn't actually my fault. But I just didn't believe it.

"Hey, Kat, got a minute?"

Startled, I looked up to see Mi Jin standing over us. She smiled at me kind of uncertainly, and my stomach dropped.

"Sure!" I left Oscar with Roland and followed her over a few rows to where she'd left her backpack on a chair. She sat next to it, and after a moment's hesitation, I sat on the other side so that the backpack was between us.

"Okay." Mi Jin took a deep breath, then unzipped her bag. "So . . . I found this in my camera bag last night."

A wave of foreboding washed over me, and I knew

what it was a split second before Mi Jin pulled it out of her backpack. Her screenplay.

She held it up, and I relaxed a tiny bit. The Thing hadn't shredded it, then. That was something. Then I saw the words scrawled in red ink over the title page.

Worst. Movie. Ever.

"Oh no," I whispered. My hands suddenly felt cold and clammy, but my face was burning hot. "Mi Jin, I . . ." But I stopped, because she had started flipping through the pages. And every single one was covered in comments. Rude, awful comments. Comments like *Terrible!* and *Ugh, seriously?* and *"My Little Pony" is scarier than this.*

Several seconds passed where I just sat there, mortified. Then I realized Mi Jin was *laughing.*

"Wait, is this . . . a joke?" I asked in disbelief. "Did you write that?"

"What? No!" she exclaimed. "No, it's just . . . well, I asked you for feedback and boy, you gave it to me."

"I didn't!" It came out so loud, I saw Dad and Jess glance up from across the gate. "I—it was . . ." I squeezed my eyes closed, trying not to cry.

"Your doppelganger?" Mi Jin said, and my eyes flew open.

"What?"

Mi Jin glanced down at the script, then back at me. "I know you, Kat. These comments . . . they're not you. I mean, they don't sound like you." My shoulders sagged in relief, but then she continued: "But thanks to all the time I've spent grading your homework, I also know your handwriting. And"—she tapped the script—"this is a match."

"Because it has my handwriting," I said desperately. "The Th . . . my doppelganger."

"Yeah, that would make sense." Mi Jin chewed her lip. "It's just . . . well, to be honest, I've noticed that ever since I gave you my script, you've been avoiding me." I ducked my head, my cheeks warm again. "And it's fine, Kat! Really. I actually thought maybe I was just imagining it. But . . ." She paused, waiting until I looked up. "Did you read it?"

"The night you gave it to me," I said quickly. "And I absolutely *loved* it."

Mi Jin smiled. "Thanks. But you had some criticism, too, right? Otherwise, you would've just told me the next day."

"I was nervous," I told her. "I—I did have some notes, but . . . I don't know. You're my teacher! Giving you notes is . . . weird. But *that*?" I pointed at the script. "Those aren't *my* notes, I swear."

"Mi Jin!" We both looked over by the water fountains where Lidia was waving, her smartphone cradled between her shoulder and her ear.

"Coming!" Mi Jin called, and we both stood up.

"Do you believe me?" I asked, hating how desperate I sounded. "I know what this looks like. Like I was too chicken to tell you all—all this." I gestured at the script in her hands. "So I just hid it in your bag and then avoided you. But I didn't write all of this, I *promise*."

I waited for Mi Jin to say *Yes, I know, of course I believe you, Kat.* But she still had that funny smile on her face, and her eyes flickered down to the script. At the words *Worst. Movie. Ever.* in what I had to admit was my exact handwriting.

"Yeah, okay," she said at last, putting a hand on my arm in what was probably supposed to be a reassuring way, but just made me feel sad and empty. "I'll, um . . . just don't worry about it, Kat."

Then she picked up her backpack and headed over to Lidia, leaving me alone. Closing my eyes, I sank back down in my chair and didn't budge until our flight started boarding twenty minutes later.

Fright TV: Your Home for Horror
Press Release: January 9

EDIE MILLS ANNOUNCES LAUNCH OF FINAL GIRL PRODUCTIONS
Former teenage Scream Queen Edie Mills, producer of the
upcoming Fright TV documentary MAGIC HOUR, today announced
the launch of Final Girl Productions. This production company will
focus on horror and dark comedies for film, television, and digital
media, and is currently accepting submissions. "No remakes or
retellings," Mills states on the company's website. "We're looking
for scripts with original concepts that break away from tired
old horror tropes. Fewer vampire vixens, more mind-bending
monsters, please."

DAD, Jess, and Lidia all stayed behind at the airport in
Seoul while the rest of us headed to our hotel. "So this
guest star's flight lands in two hours," Oscar complained as
he heaved his suitcase into the back of the van. "And you
guys *still* won't tell us who it is? Do you think Kat's going to
blab about it on her blog or something?"

"It's not a matter of trust," Roland replied, helping Mi Jin
with her bags. "It's . . . a surprise."

Oscar and I exchanged a confused glance. "Well,

obviously," I said. "It's got to be a celebrity, right?"

"Mi Jin, just tell us," Oscar begged, and she grinned.

"Nope. But trust me, you're both gonna freak out."

"Like you did?" Roland asked. "When Lidia told us who it was, you just about busted my eardrums with that scream."

Mi Jin snickered. "That's nothing. Just wait till I actually meet her in person."

"Aha! It's a her," Oscar said triumphantly. "Okay, who's Mi Jin's favorite female celebrity?"

"Beyoncé." We all turned to Sam, who was holding open the cab's passenger door. He gazed at us solemnly. "The guest star for the finale is Beyoncé." No one responded, and after a moment, Sam's brow wrinkled in confusion. "I was being sarcastic. Was that not clear?"

Roland let out a short, loud bark of laughter and walked around to the driver's side. "Clear as mud, you weirdo."

Still giggling, I climbed into the van after Oscar. We claimed the back seat, and Mi Jin slid into the seat in front of me. She squeezed her backpack between the two bucket seats, and I tried not to think about the marked-up script inside. Or the look on Mi Jin's face when I'd told her I hadn't written those notes. She wanted to believe me.

But I couldn't help worrying maybe she didn't.

Oscar and I pulled up maps on our phones, watching the blue dot that was our van leave the airport's little island and enter Seoul. When I zoomed out, I could see the Han River, which cut the city in half. Lidia had given us all an itinerary that included our hotel's address, so I mapped it. The red marker appeared on the north side of the river, right about the center of the city in a district called Itaewon. Our blue dot was way southwest of the hotel.

"Long drive," I told Oscar. We spent the next hour alternating between staring out the windows and frantically trying to find the different buildings and temples whizzing by on our maps. It turned into a competition, both of us trying to name a museum or market or particularly cool-looking skyscraper first.

By the time Roland squeezed the van into the only open spot down the street from our hotel, my stomach was growling and I seriously had to pee. As soon as Sam handed me the key cards for my room with Dad, I practically sprinted to the elevator, dragging my suitcase behind me.

Fifteen minutes later, I returned to the lobby, which was mostly empty. I sat on a stiff white armchair and pulled out my phone again, hoping Oscar would hurry up. My stomach rumbled louder than ever, and I started searching the map for restaurants close to the hotel. But a few seconds later, Mi Jin and Oscar walked in through the entrance. Each was carrying three little paper cups with plastic forks sticking out of them.

"How'd you get your stuff upstairs so fast?" I asked.

"Sam and Roland took it up while we went to find a snack," Mi Jin explained, heading to the elevator. "I'm going to bring this up to them."

Oscar sat down next to me and offered one of the paper cups. "It's called dot . . . something."

"*Ddeokbokki*!" Mi Jin called right before the elevator doors slid closed.

"What she said."

I peered into the cup. It kind of looked like the canned Chef Boyardee I loved when I was little: thick, short pasta in a bright red sauce. "Is it like spaghetti?" I asked, surprised.

"Mi Jin said they're rice dumplings." Oscar scooped up three with his fork. "It's really good. Spicy."

I stabbed one and popped it into my mouth. All thoughts of canned spaghetti instantly flew from my mind. The dumpling was soft and dense, and the sauce was a little sweet and *really* hot and absolutely nothing like Chef Boyardee. By the time we'd finished our cups and split the third, our noses were running and my eyes kept tearing up.

When Mi Jin returned with Roland and Sam, we took a walk to check out the neighborhood. A few blocks away, we found a pedestrians-only street with a market. I spotted several vendors selling more ddeokbokki, as well as steamed buns that looked similar to the ones we'd had in Beijing, and lots of other food I had no name for. There were also stalls filled with clothes, toys, and electronics, and one blindingly pink shop that sold every type of Hello Kitty product imaginable.

After Mi Jin bought a red sweater covered in little black-and-white robots, we wandered out of the market and found ourselves on a busy street lined with glass and steel skyscrapers. Roland spotted a café across the intersection, made a loud grunting noise like a zombie that caused a few passersby to stare at him in alarm, and crossed without waiting to see if the rest of us were following.

"I guess we're getting coffee," Mi Jin said with a grin.

Inside, the café was massive, and reminded me of the two-level Starbucks Jamie and Hailey had taken us to near their apartment. The menu was huge, too, and we spent almost ten minutes looking over everything before ordering: sweet-potato latte for Roland, pomegranate tea for Sam, some sort of milky, lavender-colored drink for Mi Jin, and two bubble teas (coconut for me, passion fruit for Oscar).

Roland eyed our drinks suspiciously when the barista slid them across the counter. "Yeah, I don't know if tea you can chew should be a thing that exists."

"Says the guy who ordered potato-flavored coffee," I said before slurping up a few of the chewy tapioca balls through the extra-wide straw.

"Sweet potato. Totally different." Roland's phone buzzed, and he glanced at the screen.

"They're back at the hotel!"

"*Finally.*" Oscar made a beeline for the door. I was right on his heels, and as soon as we were outside, we broke into a run. It turned into a race, both of us accidentally-on-purpose bumping into each other and trying not to spill our drinks as we sprinted down the block. I reached the hotel entrance first, but Oscar grabbed the hood of my coat just as I pushed the doors open. We stumbled into the lobby at the same time, breathless with laughter and still elbowing each other. I spotted Dad, Jess, and Lidia at the reception desk and headed for them, tossing my cup in a trash can along the way. Another woman stood facing Dad, wearing a long, stylish jacket cinched around the waist. When she turned around, I nearly tripped on the carpet.

"*Grandma?*"

She beamed, spreading her arms wide. "Surprise!"

I flew across the lobby and threw myself at her, catching a glimpse of Dad's smile right before I buried my face in Grandma's shoulder. It occurred to me that I should probably feel embarrassed about acting like a five-year-old in front of Oscar, but I didn't care. All the worry I'd been carrying about our house, Dad's future with the show, my mother, moving back to Chelsea . . . as soon as I saw Grandma, it was like all that stuff disappeared. Well, not entirely. But it suddenly felt *manageable*.

Then a horrible thought occurred to me. Had she come all the way out here because Dad told her about the stuff the Thing had done? Did Grandma think I was crazy, too?

"What are you doing here?" I asked, taking a step back.

Lidia smiled, tucking a stray strand of frizzy hair behind her ear. "You know why! Edie's going to guest star on the finale."

"But I thought the guest star was a celebrity," I blurted out. Grandma crossed her arms and gave me a mock-withering look.

"Ex*cuse* me?"

"Wow, burn," Oscar said, snickering. "On your own grandmother, too."

"No, I didn't mean..." I waved my hand. "I just... I guess I forgot you're kind of a celebrity or whatever."

"Kind of," Grandma said to Dad, who was shaking his head and grinning. "No manners, this one." She winked at me, then turned to Oscar. "Speaking of celebrities—Oscar Bettencourt. You, young man, are pretty darn captivating on camera. Have you ever considered acting?"

"Yes," Oscar replied, almost before the words were out of her mouth. "Yes, I have."

I snorted, and Lidia cleared her throat loudly. "Excuse me, what? You've never mentioned that."

"Well, you should pursue it," Grandma told Oscar firmly, and he looked so pleased I couldn't help but roll my eyes.

"Ohhhh my God," came a voice behind me. I turned to find Mi Jin gazing at Grandma and bouncing up and down on her toes. "OhmyGodohmyGodohmyGod. You're actually here."

"Mi Jin!" Grandma exclaimed, and Mi Jin froze, her mouth in a round *O*. "It's *so* good to finally meet you." She wrapped her in a hug like they were old friends, and everyone laughed at the ecstatic expression on Mi Jin's face.

She was a die-hard Edie Mills fan; I couldn't believe she'd managed to keep the fact that Grandma was the guest star a secret.

Suddenly, I felt ridiculous for not putting the pieces together sooner. Grandma was moving to L.A., producing a documentary series, getting back into film. *And* she was obsessed with *P2P*, *and* two of her family members were part of the cast. It made perfect sense for her to actually be on the show. But even though I'd seen all her movies a million times, I'd never really thought of her as a celebrity until now. She was just . . . Grandma.

The funny thing was, she even looked more like a celebrity than like a grandmother. Her clothes were straight out of *Head Turner* magazine, her makeup was perfect, and now that I looked closer, I was pretty sure she'd started dyeing the gray out of her brownish-black hair.

I hadn't seen her this glammed up in a few years, and I'd forgotten how alike she and Mom looked. Which had always struck me as weird, because their personalities couldn't have been more different.

"Edie, your production company's taking submissions, right?" Dad asked, nudging Mi Jin. "I think Mi Jin might have a script to show you."

At that, Mi Jin's face turned a nuclear shade of pink. "Oh. No. I mean, yes. I mean, I have a script, but it's—"

"It's *so good*, Grandma!" I interrupted loudly. "I read it, and the main character is awesome—she kind of reminds me of Jackie Urns in your *Asylum* movies—and it's *really* creepy. It's about doppelgangers. You should definitely read it." Mi Jin gave me a surprised but grateful smile.

"I would absolutely love to," Grandma said, and Mi Jin let out a funny little squeak that sounded like "okay." Then Grandma's eyes flickered over to the entrance, and her grin widened. "A*ha*."

I turned to see Roland and Sam tossing their empty coffee cups in the trash can by the door before heading over to us. Grandma patted at her already-perfect hair, and I was overcome with the urge to hide behind the sofa. Oh God. Oh *God*. I'd forgotten about Grandma's ridiculous crush on Sam. Not like a real crush; nothing she'd actually act on. But she definitely thought he was cute, and she wasn't shy about saying so.

"Here they are," Grandma announced, her voice somehow one thousand times throatier than usual. "The two reasons I watch *Passport to Paranormal*. No offense, Jack," she added offhandedly.

Dad tried and failed to look offended. "Yeah, thanks, Edie."

"A pleasure to meet you, Ms. Mills." Roland held out his hand, and Grandma took it. "Absolutely loved your movies when I was a kid. *My Girlfriend Is from Pluto* ruined my teenage dating life. Haven't had a girlfriend since."

"Is that so? My sincerest apologies," Grandma said, matching his solemn tone perfectly. Then she aimed her smile right at Sam. "And you? I gave my granddaughter one of my DVDs last fall hoping you'd watch it . . ."

Sam's expression remained politely blank. "Oh?"

"I didn't show it to him!" I looked at Dad for help, but he—everyone, actually—was too amused to notice my embarrassment. Except for Sam, of course. He just looked clueless, as usual.

"Well, maybe we can watch it together later," Grandma said, casually linking arms with Sam. "Actually, I really think you'd be one of the few people who'd appreciate *What She Sees in the Mirrors*. I heard your interview on Therese Koffey's radio show a few years ago, and that story you told about how you helped the woman who saw the reflection of her son who drowned every time she looked in a pool or bathtub was absolutely enchanting, it reminded me of . . ."

As she continued chatting up Sam (and batting her eyelashes *way* more than necessary), Oscar leaned closer until our arms were touching. "Your *grandmother*," he whispered. "Is *hitting*. On *Sam*."

"Shut *up*," I groaned, elbowing him in the ribs for emphasis.

"No, seriously. This is like the greatest thing that's ever happened." His voice cracked a little, and we glanced at each other, and suddenly it was just like back in Jamie and Hailey's apartment. Giggles rose up in my throat and I pressed my lips together hard to keep them in. Oscar turned around to hide his laughter, although his shaking shoulders gave it away.

"We've got a meeting in less than an hour, Edie," I heard Dad say, and Grandma finally let go of Sam's arm. "Should we get your stuff up to your room so we can grab lunch first?"

"Oh, I suppose." Grandma took the handle of her suitcase, then reached out to me with her other hand. "Help me unpack, KitKat? It'll give us a chance to catch up!"

I nodded and took her hand, still not trusting myself to speak (or look at Oscar). Dad followed us to the elevators. As soon as the doors slid closed, he turned to Grandma.

"Well," he said with a grin. "That was shameless."

Grandma waved a perfectly manicured hand. "Oh, please. I didn't embarrass you, did I, Kat?" she added, eyebrows raised.

I wrinkled my nose. "You know Sam's only interested in ghosts, right? That's what Roland always says." For some reason, that made Dad snort.

"Well, I suppose Roland would know," Grandma said, examining her fingernails. "Don't worry, sweetie. It's just a little harmless flirting."

"Extremely one-sided flirting," Dad added dryly, and Grandma swatted him lightly on the head.

As soon as Grandma opened the door to her room, my mouth fell open. "You got a *suite*?" I hurried inside, then spun around to face Dad, spreading my arms wide. "Why does Fright TV always get us the tiny rooms? This is *huge*!"

It wasn't huge, not really—the little alcove that I thought was supposed to be a living room was probably the size of Jamie and Hailey's shower—but still.

"The network knows some of us aren't so high maintenance," Dad replied, looking pointedly at Grandma. She tossed her purse onto one of the beds and untied the belt on her jacket.

"Well, that's not exactly fair," she said. "I thought I'd have a roommate, for one thing."

Dad's teasing smile disappeared, replaced with a grimace. A weird, strained silence fell between them.

"Wait . . . what's going on?" I asked. Grandma was gazing calmly at Dad, her head tilted slightly. "Hello? Who'd you think you were sharing a room with? Please don't say Sam," I added in a feeble attempt at a joke. Neither of them laughed.

Grandma slipped out of her jacket, hung it neatly on the back of the desk chair, then turned to Dad. She crossed her arms. "We talked about this in the cab, Jack," she said gently. "I told you, I'm done making excuses for her. I know you are, too."

My chest suddenly felt shrunken and tight, like it was caving in around my heart. Dad and Grandma just stood there, having a silent conversation with their eyes like they'd forgotten I was even in the room.

"Are you talking about me?" My voice shook a little, and they both turned to me at the same time.

"No! Oh, KitKat . . ." Grandma hurried over and put her arm around my shoulders. "I'm so sorry. Here, come sit down with me." She guided me to the bed by the desk. Dad spun the chair around and sat facing us. He had that look again. The defeated look I was getting tired of seeing.

"What's going on?" I asked nervously. Dad swallowed, then smiled sadly at me.

"We kept the fact that Edie was coming a secret from you because we wanted it to be a surprise," he said. "But the surprise was supposed to be . . . bigger."

"What do you mean?"

Dad's eyes flickered over to Grandma before meeting mine again. "Your mother was supposed to be here, too."

A short burst of laughter escaped me, and they both looked startled. But this had to be a joke, right? The idea of Mom here in Seoul, hanging around the *Passport to Paranormal* crew . . . it was like trying to picture Captain America in Arendelle. Didn't fit. Different worlds. Wrong, wrong, wrong.

"Wait, seriously?" I asked. "Why?" As soon as I said it, the answer hit me. Because Dad thought I'd torn up his contract. Because he thought I wanted to be with Mom. I opened my mouth to argue, but Grandma spoke first.

"Because I pushed her to," she said. "Your mother left almost a year ago, Kat. Since then, you've seen her once—at Thanksgiving, when you and Jack visited. And you agreed to come to her shower in March, too. You shouldn't be the only one who . . . who makes an effort."

I didn't respond. I had absolutely no idea what to say to that. I didn't even know what Grandma meant.

"So when I told her last month that I was joining you in Seoul," Grandma went on, placing her hand gently on my back. "I asked her to come. She said yes. I bought her plane ticket and made all the arrangements . . ." She sighed. "Then yesterday, she called and said there'd been an emergency. A wedding planning emergency, nothing serious," she added quickly when my eyes widened in alarm. "Something about the caterer, I don't know . . . but I *do* know it couldn't possibly have been so urgent it couldn't wait a week."

A strange new mix of emotions started churning through me. The same hurt I always felt when Mom did stuff like this. But also, relief. Grandma's disappointment in my mother was obvious. She blamed *Mom*, not me. It didn't lessen the hurt, but it was weirdly comforting.

Dad shifted in his chair. "I'm sorry, Kat," he said quietly. "I wasn't sure about telling you, but your grandma insisted."

"We're being honest," Grandma told him. "I don't need you guilt-tripping yourself anymore, either. I swear, between the two of you—"

"What do you feel guilty about?" I interrupted, staring at Dad.

A muscle twitched in his cheek. "Talking about your mother like this with you. Ever since she left, I've . . . I never wanted you to feel like you had to choose sides. I didn't want the fact that *I* was upset with her to upset *you.*"

I blinked. "She's the one who left. Why would I be upset with you?"

"No, I mean later," Dad said. "When she moved back to Chelsea. When I'd invite her over to see you and she wouldn't come. When she told me she'd gotten engaged and asked *me* to tell you, instead of doing it herself."

My throat felt dry and scratchy. "I didn't want to talk to her then, though. I wouldn't, when she called."

"I know." Dad smiled sadly at me. "But, sweetie, she could have tried harder. Six months was a long time. I can't imagine going that long without seeing you . . . you're my *daughter.* I would've found a way. I think I put that burden on you, when it was really your mother's fault the two of you weren't talking." He wrinkled his nose. "Ugh, see? I feel guilty just saying that. Father of the year, like everyone's saying."

I barely heard what he said after *your mother's fault.* Dad blamed Mom, too. He blamed her for how long we'd gone last year without speaking. And he was right—I *had* thought that was my fault. I'd thought Grandma and Dad thought that was my fault, too. Mom called every few weeks, and I'd refuse to talk. That was it.

It had never dawned on me that maybe she should have tried harder.

"Well, I don't feel guilty at all about saying this to both of you." Grandma paused, sitting up straighter. "I love my

134

daughter. She's a beautiful, talented woman with many wonderful qualities. But she can also be very, *very* selfish."

We were silent for a moment. I kept waiting for tears, but I was . . . okay. Not happy. Not sad. But okay.

"And," Grandma added, "Shelly Mathers better hope she never meets me, because I have a thing or two to say to her about that father of the year business."

"What father of the year business?" I asked, looking from her to Dad.

Dad rolled his eyes. "Her review of the Beijing episode. She had a few unflattering opinions about me using my daughter as a publicity stunt. Or putting her life in danger by exposing her to a deadly doppelganger," he added dryly. "Whichever it is . . . she's not sure. Either way, a whole lot of people apparently think I'm a terrible father. I've got some trolls of my own now."

Aaaand here came the guilt again. But this time, I was right to blame myself. "I shouldn't have joked about dying on the finale," I said. "It was . . . I didn't think about what people would say about you. I'm sorry."

"It's not like we couldn't have edited it out," Dad told me. "But we didn't anticipate so many viewers taking it so seriously . . . as if I'd actually put your life in danger. Point is, it's not your fault, sweetie."

I tried to smile at him, but I knew he was wrong. And not just about it being my fault.

I might actually be in danger. I hadn't thought about it

until Dad said it, but so far, everything the Thing had done had been to try to convince Dad to move back to Chelsea. He was pretty much ready to do it, too. If something bad happened to me on the finale, that might be just the push he needed.

Chapter Twelve
SO YOU THINK YOU CAN BLOG

P2P WIKI
Entry: "Poltergeist"
[Last edited by Maytrix]

A poltergeist is a particularly wicked type of ghost intent on wreaking havoc on anyone who comes into its space. Unlike ghosts, they are not typically human in origin, and reasons for their manifestations can vary greatly.

AFTER a late lunch, Dad and Grandma headed out with Jess and Lidia to conduct a few interviews about the asylum we'd be investigating tomorrow. Oscar and I did a short algebra lesson with Mi Jin, who seemed a little distracted. After giving us an essay assignment for social studies, she pulled out her laptop and started typing furiously, brow furrowed. Working on her screenplay, I realized with a pang of guilt. She was probably nervous about showing it to Grandma. And the Thing's notes couldn't have boosted her confidence.

"Time!" she said an hour later, snapping her laptop closed. "Hand 'em over."

Oscar and I dutifully handed her our papers. I turned to

Oscar, tossing my pen down on the desk.

"Grandma's suite has a pretty nice TV. Want to see if anything good's on?"

"Um . . ." Oscar glanced at the time on his phone. "Maybe later? I'm gonna use Aunt Lidia's laptop while she's out."

"'Kay." I stifled a yawn. "Text me when you're done. Bye, Mi Jin."

"Bye, Kat!" Mi Jin gave me a quick smile before turning back to her screenplay.

Up in the suite, I kicked off my shoes and dumped my bag on the couch before flopping down on Grandma's bed. Five minutes later, I'd found what looked like a pretty decent Korean horror movie with English subtitles. Five minutes after that, I was sound asleep.

The next thing I knew, a shriek woke me up with a jolt. Disoriented, I stared frantically around the suite before remembering the movie. On the TV screen, a screaming girl was climbing a ladder with some sort of grayish demon-creature right on her heels. I grabbed the remote and hit mute, then tried to go to sleep again.

But adrenaline was still racing through my veins. I lay perfectly still, watching the demon claw at the girl's calves and eventually drag her down into the darkness below, listening to my too-quick heartbeat. Then I realized that wasn't the only sound I could hear.

Click. Click-clack click click. Click.

I didn't move. Just looked slowly, deliberately around

the room, searching for the source of the soft clicking. My eyes fell on the laptop, which sat open on the desk. The dashboard to my blog was on the screen, opened to a new post. Words I couldn't see from here were appearing in the blank space.

Someone—some*thing*—was typing.

An odd calmness settled over me. My pulse slowed, my hands were cool and dry. Quietly, stealthily, I slipped out of bed and tiptoed over to the couch. I pulled the Elapse out of my bag and flipped it on, making sure it was in video mode before making my way over to the desk.

I trod as softly as possible, my eyes flickering between the laptop in the viewfinder and the laptop itself. As I closed in, I could read the words in the blog post. Just two words, typed over and over again.

SAVE YOURSELF SAVE YOURSELF SAVE YOURSELF SAVE YOURSELF
SAVE YOURSELF SAVE YOURSELF SAVE YOURSELF SAVE YOURSELF
SAVE YOURSELF SAVE YOURSELF SAVE YOURSELF SAVE YOURSELF
SAVE YOURSELF SAVE YOURSELF

It was mesmerizing, watching letter after letter appear. So mesmerizing that several seconds passed before I noticed movement in my peripheral vision. I glanced at the mirror, and my breath caught in my chest.

The Thing sat at the desk, typing methodically on the laptop. It was wearing a nightgown this time, its long braid—the one I'd cut off, the one my mother loved—

hanging over its shoulder. It didn't notice me at all; or if it did, it didn't show it.

I took a step to the side, framing the whole scene in the viewfinder. The empty chair in front of me. The other version of me in the mirror. And the reflection of me, the real me, next to it, capturing both of us on camera.

This was unreal. It was even more shocking than the footage Jess got on the bridge. Me and my "doppelganger," side by side.

A few seconds later, the Thing stopped typing. It stood, and I took another step back. I watched the mirror closely as it walked past me, turning to capture as much of it as possible before it disappeared beyond the frame. I hurried to the other side of the mirror, but it was gone.

My hands trembled as I removed the memory card from my camera and slid it into the laptop. As the video uploaded, I scrolled down to the bottom of the blog post. After thinking for a moment, I added:

Everything above this was written by my doppelganger. It's been leaving comments online for the last few weeks as "The Real Kat Sinclair." Watch video below for proof.

Once the video was embedded, I hit play. And there it was, clear as day. Two Kats, captured on video. I almost laughed out loud. No one could say this was faked. Well, they could try. But this wasn't a blurry image in a photo or a two-second shot of a girl surrounded by fog who looked like me if you squinted. Faking something like this would be expensive. The muted horror movie still playing out on the TV didn't even have special effects as good as what I had captured just now.

I let the arrow hover over *Publish*, then frowned. One of the adults, usually Dad or Lidia, had to approve my posts before I could publish them. As much as I wanted to put this blog post up now, I had to wait.

I hit *Save Draft*, then shot a quick text to Oscar.

KS: Come to Grandma's suite NOW!

I waited nearly a minute, then remembered how eager he'd been to use Lidia's laptop. Quickly, I opened video chat and spotted the green *Online* dot next to Oscar's name. He was probably talking to Thiago.

Sighing, I started to close the window, but another green dot caught my eye. I glanced at the time and did a little quick math in my head. It was a bit after three in the morning in New York; he couldn't actually be online . . . right?

Only one way to find out. I clicked *Call* next to Jamie's avatar and waited, holding my breath. After nearly ten seconds of ringing, the window suddenly expanded—and there was Jamie, rubbing his eyes, hair sticking out all over the place.

"Kat?"

"Sorry, were you sleeping?" I asked stupidly. "I mean, I know it's late there—or, um, early—but I noticed you were online and, uh . . . something kind of weird happened? And I need to talk to someone about it."

Now Jamie looked wide awake. "The Thing again?"

"Yeah." I launched into the story, the words spilling out of me. The more I talked, the more tired I felt. Not just tired. *Exhausted.* Like every single one of my bones was increasing in density. My vision kept blurring, and when I blinked, my eyelashes seemed to be weights, pulling my eyelids down.

"And you recorded all of it?" Jamie asked eagerly. "You checked the video?"

"Yeah, it's even better than . . ." I trailed off, yawning hugely. "Sorry. Better than what Jess got on the bridge."

Jamie frowned. "Are you okay? You look like you're about to pass out."

"I'm fine, just really sleepy."

"Isn't it, like, the middle of the day there?"

"Mmhmm." I could see Jamie's bed behind him. Curling up under a pile of blankets seemed like the most inviting thing in the world. "Sorry again for waking you up."

"Don't be," Jamie said. "This is exactly why I left video chat open."

"For . . ." I paused for another gigantic yawn. "For me to creep you out in the middle of the night?"

"Well, yeah." After a second's hesitation, he added: "What are boyfriends for?"

The word *boyfriend* took a moment to register. A blush crept up my neck, and I realized he was smiling kind of nervously, waiting for me to respond.

"For emergency doppelganger sightings, I guess," I said, smiling back at him. "Straight out of a sappy romance movie."

Jamie laughed, then stopped when I yawned yet again. "Seriously, why are you so tired?"

"I don't . . ." I covered my mouth with my arm as another yawn hit. ". . . know. I was taking a nap when the Thing showed up. I just need to . . . to lie down for a sec . . ."

I couldn't fight my eyelids anymore. Jamie was saying something as I rested my head on my arms and closed my eyes. "Just for a sec," I murmured again, and sank into a deep sleep.

CHAPTER THIRTEEN

THE ZOMBIE AWAKENS

From: trishhhhbequiet@mymail.net
To: acciopancakes@mymail.net, timelord2002@mymail.net
Subject: That blog post

um. are you ok? mark and I are kinda worried . . .

From: acciopancakes@mymail.net
To: trishhhhbequiet@mymail.net, timelord2002@mymail.net
Subject: Re: That blog post

I'll be fine once I'm back home where I belong. With my mother.

WAKING up was like trying to climb out of quicksand. I struggled to reach consciousness, fighting against vague dreams of dark creatures pulling and clawing at my legs. When I finally pried my eyes open, it took a few seconds for them to adjust.

This wasn't my hotel room. Or my bed.

And someone was in the room with me.

The memory of what had happened before I'd fallen asleep hit me, and I sat up with a gasp, like I'd been slapped in the face. Over in the desk chair, Grandma glanced up, very clearly startled.

"Well, good morning, sunshine!" she exclaimed. "I was going to give you five more minutes before trying cold water."

Disoriented, I took in the sunshine streaming in between the curtains, the fact that Grandma was wearing different clothes than she had been when I last saw her, the tiny coffeepot brewing on the desk next to the open laptop.

"It's . . . morning?" I asked groggily. "Did I spend the whole night here?"

Grandma chuckled. "You did indeed. Fell asleep talking to a young man online . . . your father had some words to say about that, I can tell you."

"Jamie," I said, suddenly feeling a little panicked. "I . . . fell asleep while I was talking to him?"

"Mmhmm," Grandma said. "He was worried, so he got in touch with Oscar, who came up here and found you conked out at the desk."

"And he . . . told Dad?" I asked, trying to put the pieces together.

"Oscar woke you up," Grandma said. "And apparently, you were quite irritated. *A cranky zombie,* I believe, were his exact words. You got into my bed and no one could wake you for the world. Lucky for me, that couch turned out to be quite comfortable."

I rubbed my eyes, then squinted at her. Despite her light

tone and easy smile, I could tell Grandma was trying to hide the fact that she was worried. Then I saw my blog on the laptop screen. Two words jumped out, and my blood went cold.

SAVE YOURSELF

"Is that . . . d-did it . . ." I stuttered, crawling forward on the bed. "That blog post, is it . . . published?"

Grandma took a deep breath. "You published it last night, yes."

"No, I didn't." I sat back on my heels. "I didn't, I hit save, then I called Jamie . . ." But there was no use defending myself. Apparently, the Thing wanted its post and video out there. Swallowing, I looked at Grandma. "Were Dad and Lidia mad?"

"No, sweetie. Not mad." Grandma reached out, brushing a strand of hair off my forehead. "Just . . . concerned."

"Because of the . . . my doppelganger." I was wide awake now. What did the fans think? Were they saying even worse stuff about Dad? "I know what Mi Jin says about doppelgangers, but I don't think I'm actually going to *die*, I shouldn't have said that, I . . ." I took a deep breath and sat up straighter. This was it. Time to tell the truth. Grandma watched me, her eyes filled with worry.

"It's not a doppelganger. It's an artificial ghost," I told her. "Like Brunilda Cano, the ghost of a possessed nun that

146

Professor Guzmán created. And Roland! He made one when he was a boy, the ghost of a librarian who was never real—his brother made up the whole thing. And mine, the one in the video, it's . . ." I wanted to say it. I was going to say it. "It's . . ."

"Kat," Grandma whispered. "Sweetheart. There's no ghost in this video."

I blinked. "What? Of course there is."

Pursing her lips, Grandma reached out and touched the trackpad, moving the arrow over to the play button. She hesitated for just a moment before clicking.

On the screen, I saw the Korean horror movie playing on the TV. I saw the desk, the laptop, the dashboard for my blog. I saw the mirror, and I saw my reflection, holding the camera, staring at an empty chair.

Numbness spread through my limbs. "No, that's not . . ." I squeezed my eyes closed briefly, then stared hard at the screen, willing the Thing to appear. "It was *there*. I watched this video last night; it was *there*. You could see it in the mirror."

Before Grandma could respond, I quickly scrambled off the bed and paused the video. Then I scrolled up to the top of the post. It was all there, all the *Save yourselves*, and my message underneath it. My message that made me sound like a complete, certifiable nutjob. Because now it looked like I had typed up this whole nonsensical post, then added a video of my own reflection watching an empty chair through my camera.

There were 168 comments so far. I couldn't even bring myself to read them.

"Everyone thinks I'm crazy," I said dully. "Don't they."

"Oh, sweetheart." Grandma placed a finger under my chin, tilting my head back and looking me in the eyes. "No one thinks you're crazy. But I won't pretend we aren't . . . confused. Your father says he's tried to talk to you about your actions lately. Ripping up his contract, leaving those comments on your mother's Facebook—"

"I didn't do any of that!" I cried. "It was the Thing. Wait—I can prove it."

Grandma's brows furrowed as I flew off the bed and across the room, grabbing my backpack off the couch. After dumping the contents on the floor, I frantically dug through the mess until I found it: the flash drive.

"*Ha*," I said triumphantly, marching back over to the laptop. "Remember when I e-mailed you about being camera shy? You told me to practice getting comfortable on camera by myself. So I did." I inserted the flash drive as I spoke, then opened the video. "Watch the mirror."

"No one's going to see this. Ever."

I crossed my arms, staring at myself standing in the hotel room back in Salvador. Grandma sat perfectly still next to me. My heart pounded faster and my palms started to sweat as the clip got closer to the part where the Thing first appeared. I hadn't known that's what it was at first, but it was there. A blurry shape in the mirror. I leaned forward in anticipation.

"Just. Freaking. Relax."

The video ended, frozen on a frame of my hand grabbing the camera. I couldn't believe my eyes.

Nothing.

No.

Thing.

"No, it was *there*," I hissed, clicking back to play the final few seconds again. I glared at the mirror, willing the blur to happen, praying I'd missed it somehow the first time. But there was absolutely no movement behind video-me.

I'd never shown anyone this video because I was too embarrassed. But now I wish I'd just gotten over it. Because the Thing had been *there*. And now it wasn't.

"Kat, honey," Grandma was saying, but I ignored her. This was like . . . like the opposite of thoughtography. Instead of projecting a ghost onto a video, I'd *removed* one. Two, actually. But I sure as hell hadn't done it on purpose. *The world's first accidental reverse psychic photographer,* I thought, and almost laughed out loud.

Only I didn't really believe that. No, this was the Thing's doing. It must have been. It was trying to make me look crazy so that Dad would leave the show and we'd go back to Chelsea. And every time I asked for help or tried to tell someone the truth—Grandma, Dad, the entire *Passport to Paranormal* fandom—I just looked crazier.

Enough of that. If I was going to beat the Thing, I had to do it on my own.

"Never mind," I told Grandma, getting to my feet abruptly and pocketing the flash drive. "Wrong video. And the blog post . . . it was supposed to be a joke. I was tired, seemed like a good idea. I'll apologize to the crew." Grandma opened her mouth, but I continued. "Meet you downstairs for breakfast, okay? I'm gonna go back to my room and take a shower."

And I grabbed my bag and left the room without looking back at her.

THE TRUTH ISN'T OUT THERE

**Post: Ryang Jeongsin Byeong-won (Ryang Psychiatric Hospital)
Comments (231)**

Hi, everyone! This is Oscar, temporarily taking over Kat's blog. She's fine, she's just taking a break from the Internet for a while.

For the season finale of *P2P*, we're in Seoul investigating the Ryang Psychiatric Hospital. It's been abandoned, but very recently, so it probably won't look quite as creepy as Daems Prison or the catacombs in Buenos Aires. The patients and staff were all moved to a new, better facility in another neighborhood, and this hospital was purchased by a production company based here in Seoul. They want to use the building as a setting for a movie about a haunted asylum, and since this place is rumored to be haunted, they thought it would make the film more authentic if they filmed here.

Supposedly, the hospital has its very own poltergeist. A really angry, really noisy one. There's a rumor that back when the hospital opened decades ago, some nurse accidentally opened a portal and let in the poltergeist . . . which means it was never human.

So what IS it? Stay tuned to watch us try to find out!

OSCAR might have had potential as an actor, but I was giving him a run for his money. The second I joined the rest of the crew in the hotel lobby, I started putting on the performance of a lifetime.

I apologized to Dad and everyone for the *Save Yourself* post. Yes, I knew I was supposed to get all posts approved. No, of course I didn't actually think my doppelganger had written it. Yes, I knew the video didn't show anything remotely paranormal—it was supposed to be a joke! Just trying to lighten things up after my whole "will I die in the season finale" mistake, bad judgment on my part, ha-ha, won't happen again.

No one bought the act at first, especially not Dad or Grandma. But I stuck to it, smiling and calmly eating my pastry, until finally Lidia changed the subject and started talking about our itinerary for the day. We were going to spend the morning filming in the neighborhood where the psychiatric hospital was located. The people from the production company who had bought the facility were going to meet us, and Grandma would be conducting most of the interviews. Then we'd return to the hotel for dinner, pack up, and head back out to spend the night in the hospital.

Oscar caught on to what I was doing right away. The trip across town took about half an hour, and we spent the whole time joking around in the back of the van, ignoring the occasional concerned glances from the adults.

When we pulled up to Ryang Psychiatric Hospital, a group of people was standing outside of the entrance, all smiling eagerly. I felt a brief wave of déjà vu, remembering the fans who had found us at the Montgomery. Lidia was the first out of the van, and a guy with longish graying hair pulled into a ponytail stepped forward.

"Ms. Bettencourt!" he exclaimed, his words carrying the slightest hint of an accent. "We spoke on the phone earlier. I'm Jae-Hwa."

"So nice to finally meet you in person!" Lidia shook his hand, then turned to Dad and Jess, who were right behind her. "Park Jae-Hwa. He's the founder of Talchul Films."

A blur of introductions followed, during which Oscar and I hung back. Jae-Hwa's whole staff—five people, including him—all seemed excited to meet the crew, and *really* excited to meet Grandma. They weren't so interested in Oscar and me, which was a relief—and, well, maybe a little bit of a surprise, too. After my unfortunate blog post, *P2P* fans had been arguing nonstop in the forums about whether or not we were just faking the whole doppelganger thing. But maybe in real life, no one cared whether my double would try to attack me during the finale. Not even the people who owned the place we'd be investigating.

After several minutes of chatting, we all trooped inside the hospital. I blinked in surprise, nudging Oscar.

"You weren't kidding about this place," I told him. "It's not creepy at all."

The lobby was still furnished with a few sofas and chairs. A flat-screen TV hung on the wall, although I could see the cables dangling from the back. A few filing cabinets sat against the wall behind the receptionist's desk, and there were even a few magazines still stacked neatly on a little table in the corner.

"Did they leave all the furniture?" Roland asked, glancing down the hall to the left. "Beds, all that stuff in the rooms?"

Jae-Hwa nodded. "The hospital's new facility included an upgrade in equipment. When we bought this building, we asked that the owners include all of the furnishings they no longer needed in the price. For us, it was a ready-made set for our first film."

"Nice," Grandma murmured thoughtfully as she gazed around. I could practically see the wheels turning in her head, probably thinking about her own production company and whatever its first movie would be. I breathed a small sigh of relief; for a few hours, at least, she and Dad would be focused on something aside from their concern that I was losing my mind.

"Kat, check this out." Oscar waved me over to the hallway, where he stood by the first door. "Looks like a nurses' lounge or something." We both glanced at the adults, who were all getting settled on the sofas and chairs in the lobby. Jess and Mi Jin were setting up their cameras, while Dad pinned microphones on Jae-Hwa and Grandma. I caught Dad's eye and pointed to the lounge. After a second's hesitation, he nodded, and Oscar and I hurried inside and closed the door.

"Finally," Oscar said, turning to me expectantly. "Jamie

already told me everything, but I want to hear it from you. What happened, exactly?"

So I told him about the soft clicking on the laptop, watching the same two words appear over and over again on the screen, seeing the Thing in the mirror, long braid hanging over its shoulder. I told him how it had stood and walked out of sight, and how I'd sat down to video chat with Jamie and ended up dozing off.

"It's too bad you didn't show Jamie the video," Oscar mused.

I glanced up. "Why?"

"Just, you know ..." he shrugged, looking uncomfortable. "So another person would've seen it."

"So you'd know whether or not I'm going crazy," I said flatly.

Oscar sighed. "That's not what I said."

I squeezed my hands into fists so hard my knuckles turned white. "So you believe me? You believe it was on my camera?"

Oscar shifted in his chair, opened his mouth, then closed it again. I raised my eyebrows expectantly, and he sighed.

"Okay. Look, Kat, I *do* believe you. But—"

I groaned, closing my eyes. This was it. The last straw. Even *Oscar* thought I was losing it.

"No, listen," he said, leaning forward. "The Thing *is* real. We all saw it on the bridge, and on video. I don't know what happened to the video you got last night, but that doesn't change the fact that literally everyone has seen a ghost that looks exactly like you. *That* one's still on video, the one Jess got."

"But?"

"But . . ." Oscar paused. "When you told me what happened to your dad's contract, you said you'd had a weird dream the night before about him getting mad at you. And yesterday, when I came up to the suite and woke you up— you don't even remember that! And you said when you saw the Thing, you'd just woken up from a nap, and then you got really drowsy again. So maybe you're, like . . . sleepwalking. Or something."

"You mean sleep blog-posting," I said dully. "Sleep ripping up contracts. Sleep writing rude comments all over Mi Jin's script, too?"

Oscar sighed, clearly frustrated. "Look, don't get all defensive. I already said I know the Thing is real—I don't think you're making this stuff up. But maybe some of the stuff that's happened is . . ."

"Is me," I finished. "And I only think it's the Thing. You know, this is a lot like what you said to me about Sonja when we were in Rotterdam. You believed I thought I was telling the truth. But that's not the same as actually believing me." I knew I should stop talking, that Oscar was just trying to help. But I was frustrated, too. "And that was before we were even friends. I thought you trusted me, but I guess I was wrong."

"We *are* friends," Oscar snapped. "I'm being honest with you. That's what actual friends do, not just agree with you even when you might be wrong."

I crossed my arms and half-shrugged. He was right, which just irritated me even more.

"And besides, think about this," Oscar went on, his tone slightly softer. "You made the Thing, right? It came from your head. Maybe it can . . . get back in there sometimes. Make you do stuff without you realizing it."

I sat up straighter. "You mean possess me?"

"Maybe?" Oscar's brow furrowed. "We thought you were possessed in Buenos Aires. You had all those weird symptoms. And then the Thing . . . came out. Came out of *you*. So it's kind of like you were possessed. Maybe it still has a connection with you or something."

"Huh."

"And . . ." Oscar tilted his head. "And your camera."

"My camera?"

"The Thing is still on Jess's video," he said. "Taken on Jess's camera. It's only your camera it keeps disappearing from."

We fell silent, listening to the muffled sounds of voices in the lobby. The more I thought about what Oscar had said, the more it made sense. Especially about the Elapse. My love of photography was pretty much the only thing I'd ever had in common with my mom. The Thing was the version of me that had *everything* in common with my mom. In a twisted way, it made sense that it'd be able to worm its way in and out of my photography, but no one else's.

For months, I'd been trying to find an explanation for the Thing. An artificial ghost, thoughtography . . . but if there was one thing I'd learned since joining *P2P*, it was that there was hardly ever a definitive explanation for paranormal activity. Just theories and ideas.

Maybe the Thing was something new entirely.

CHAPTER FIFTEEN
FOR THE LOVE OF BODY DOUBLES

From: acciopancakes@mymail.net
To: jamiebaggins@mymail.net
Subject: Hello

I know we talked about visiting each other over the summer.
However, that will not be possible since I'm moving back to
Chelsea to be with my mother and I don't plan on leaving ever
again. Also, graveyards and creepy museums are not ideal places
to take girlfriends. I'm sorry for leading you on.

From: acciopancakes@mymail.net
To: jamiebaggins@mymail.net
Subject: Re: Hello

Jamie, I'm so sorry. I didn't write that e-mail, I swear. I think
maybe I figured out what's going on. Can we video chat soon?
SORRY AGAIN!!!
Kat (the actual real one, not the fake one who says she's the real
one)

AFTER a long lunch with everyone from Talchul Films
at a restaurant near the hospital, the *P2P* crew headed
back to our hotel to get ready for tonight's investigation.
Oscar and I packed our backpacks quickly and went

159

down to the lobby together.

"Don't worry, Jamie'll believe you," Oscar said. "That e-mail didn't sound like you at all."

I made a face. "I hope so. If the Thing's going to keep doing this, maybe I should just delete my e-mail account. And my blog. And just . . . not exist online, at all."

"That's the most ridiculous thing you've ever said."

I let out a little laugh as the elevator doors slid open. But honestly, the thought was tempting.

"KitKat, come over here!" Grandma called from the sofa, where she sat with Mi Jin. "You said you read Mi Jin's screenplay, right?"

I winced, trying not to picture the horrible comments in my handwriting that covered the script. "Yeah, I did."

"And I'd like to know what you *really* thought," Mi Jin said, winking at me. "I know you said you liked it, but I get the sense that maybe you have some suggestions?"

Grandma patted the spot next to her on the sofa, and I sat down tentatively. Oscar flopped down in the armchair opposite Mi Jin and gave me a look that clearly said *Don't be a chicken.*

"Okay," I said. "Well, I guess it was the part where the main character—Lee, right?—when she actually sees her doppelganger face-to-face for the first time. She screams and runs, like she's really shocked. But . . . but that doesn't really make sense."

Mi Jin nodded encouragingly. "How so?"

"Because there were all these signs before then that something weird was going on," I replied. "Like finding that burned figurine, and when she felt like someone was watching her in the scene at her grandmother's funeral. There were other clues, too . . . so by the time she sees her doppelganger, I get that it's still scary. But not surprising. She knew something was up."

"Huh." Mi Jin nodded, a smile spreading slowly across her face. "That makes a lot of sense, actually."

"Indeed it does," Grandma agreed, and I noticed for the first time that she was holding a copy of the script. (Thankfully, it appeared to be a clean copy with no mean notes.) "The way you've described it, it sounds like her doppelganger has been lurking around for quite a while prior to the start of the story. It reminds me of the stalker I dealt with when I was a teenager."

Oscar's eyes widened. "You had a stalker? Like . . . Emily with Sam?"

"I sure did," Grandma said lightly. "I started receiving letters from him after *Vampires of New Jersey* came out. By the time I was filming *Return to the Asylum*, things had gotten out of hand. I knew something bad was coming—I could feel it. So when the kidnapping happened, well . . . it's like Kat said. I was horrified, but not surprised."

"You were *kidnapped*?" I blurted out. Grandma had mentioned her stalker before, but I'd never gotten any details out of her.

"Not me. My stunt double. Sandra."

She sat quietly for a few seconds, a small, sad smile tugging at the corners of her mouth. I waited, hoping she'd continue. Mi Jin and Oscar were watching her, too. I was pretty sure all three of us were holding our breaths.

Finally, Grandma spoke. "Sandra started working for me during *Cannibal Clown Circus*. I played an acrobat . . . it was the first role I ever had where I needed a stunt double. Up close, we didn't look terribly similar. But we were around the same height and weight, and with a little hair dye, from a distance . . ." She trailed off, her eyes distant. "Well. It was easy to confuse us."

I sat perfectly still, watching her. I couldn't believe Grandma had never told me this story before.

"Well, one day we were at the studio till well after midnight," she went on softly. "I was on edge—this was after five weeks of filming *Return to the Asylum*, and on top of that the letters from my stalker had gotten more frequent, and more disturbing. Sandra and I usually left the studio together, with my bodyguard. This was the second movie we had worked on together, and we were close. Spent all our time together. But our friendship was . . . well . . . it was intense. We loved each other, but we fought over the most ridiculous things. We had had another squabble that day, I can't even remember over what. When we finished filming, I went and sulked in my dressing room until she left."

Her mouth tightened, and a feeling of foreboding

washed over me. Oscar had paled slightly, and he gazed at Grandma without blinking.

"He was lurking outside the studio, waiting for me." Grandma sighed. "He saw me without my bodyguard—or at least, he thought he did—and seized the opportunity. Sandra never saw him coming. He snuck up behind her, dragged her into his car, drove off . . . by the time he realized his mistake, they were far from the studio. None of us even realized she was missing until the next morning when she didn't show up to work."

"Did you . . . did they find her?" Mi Jin asked. I wasn't sure I wanted to hear the answer, and I could tell from his expression that Oscar felt the same.

Grandma blinked, her eyes coming into focus. "Yes! Yes, I'm sorry, I didn't mean to imply . . ." She waved her hand. "The police tracked them down in a few days, holed up in a little apartment about an hour from the studio. Sandra was unharmed . . . well, physically. But she was traumatized. Had no more interest in being my body double, for obvious reasons." Grandma paused. "Our relationship was never the same after that. I blamed myself for what happened to her. Still do."

I glanced at Oscar. "It wasn't your fault, obviously. It was the stalker."

"Well, of course I know that, sweetie," Grandma said with a smile, bumping my shoulder with hers. "But I couldn't help playing the *what if* game. What if I hadn't sulked in my dressing room and let her leave the studio alone? What if I hadn't fought with her that day at all? What if I'd gone to the police sooner with those letters, instead of convincing myself for so long that my stalker was just a particularly enthusiastic 'fan'?" She spread out her hands. "Sandra never would have gone through such a dreadful ordeal."

At some point, Mi Jin had pulled out a notebook, and she was scribbling furiously. Grandma arched her eyebrows. "Taking notes, dear?"

Mi Jin looked up, blushing. "Oh! No, not about Sandra. Just, like . . ." She gestured at the screenplay in Grandma's lap. "Between your story and all that stuff Kat said, I have some revision ideas, and I wanted to get them down before I forget."

"Wonderful!" Grandma handed her the script. "Why don't I hold off on reading this until you've revised? We'll consider it an official submission for Final Girl Productions."

I couldn't help snickering at the way Mi Jin's eyes bulged. "What. Seriously. Um. Yes?"

"Excellent." The elevator doors opened, and Roland and Jess appeared, loaded down with bags and equipment. Grandma stood, smoothing down her blouse. "Looks like we're about ready to head out!"

I stood, too, picking up my backpack and waiting until Grandma and Mi Jin were busy helping the rest of the crew. Oscar was still in the armchair, staring blankly at the sofa. I gently nudged his leg with my foot. "You okay?"

He jumped slightly and looked up at me. "What? Yeah. Fine."

"Guess you're not the only one who plays the *what if* game," I said, keeping my voice as casual as possible. Oscar tried to look annoyed and failed.

"Yeah," he said, shouldering his backpack. "I guess not."

CHAPTER SIXTEEN
KNOCK, KNOCK

P2P WIKI
Entry: "Portal"
[Last edited by AntiSimon]

In paranormal studies, the term *portal* generally means a doorway between our physical world and the spirit world. Portals can theoretically allow spirits to enter our world, and humans to enter the spirit world. In season 1, episode 13, of *Passport to Paranormal*, the crew visited Blacksmith Bar in New Orleans, which the owners claimed was the site of a portal haunting, letting in restless, occasionally angry spirits. Sam Sumners attempted to close the portal, with inconclusive results.

RYANG Psychiatric Hospital was eerie in an entirely different way from any other location I'd explored with *Passport to Paranormal*. Crimptown and the catacombs had been dark and cramped and deep underground. Daems Penitentiary was a classic horror movie setting—an enormous, concrete structure in the middle of nowhere. The waterfall in Salvador was beautiful, but exploring the woods in the dead of night gave you the feeling that someone was always watching, hidden in the dark just out of sight. And the fog swirling around the Yongheng Bridge, not to mention the sheer drops into a black abyss, made it an undeniably spooky setting.

In contrast, fluorescent lights blazed in the hallways of the hospital. No spiderwebs or decades' worth of grime; every room was scrubbed clean and smelled like bleach. The beds were neatly made, and the shelves were still stocked with medical equipment. I knew the Talchul Films crew had kept it this way on purpose, but the overall impression was that the entire staff and all the patients had vanished into thin air just moments ago. The deserted yet clinical atmosphere made me picture some evil doctor lurking in one of the empty rooms, scalpel in hand, waiting for his next "patient."

It might have been my imagination, but everyone seemed to be keeping a closer eye on me than usual. When I lingered behind in the doctors' lounge for a few seconds to see if the TV worked (it didn't), I found Roland just outside the door tying his shoe. When I stepped inside the pantry in the kitchen, Lidia followed me even though she'd already checked it out a few minutes earlier. By the time we got up to the second floor, I was pretty irritated and half considering hiding out in a room by myself for a minute or two, just to get some privacy. But that would be breaking Dad's number one rule for these investigations, and I didn't need to give him any more reasons to quit the show.

Although at the moment, he didn't look like a man who was unhappy with his job. Pretty much the exact opposite.

After four months and five episodes, he'd developed an easy rapport with Roland and Sam on camera. And he and Grandma were the perfect cohosts—no surprise, at least not to me. I'd watched countless horror movies with the two of them, and their commentary and arguments with each other over plot twists and special effects were always hilarious.

I tried to imagine him having this much fun on *Live with Wendy* and . . . there was just no way. Dad loved this job. He really, really loved it. I couldn't let him quit because of me.

No, not because of me. Because of the Thing.

"Now *this* brings back memories," Grandma announced when we entered the director's office. She immediately walked over to the desk and sat behind it, clasping her hands and surveying the rest of us imperiously. "About half the scenes I filmed in *The Asylum* took place in the Warden's office. Camera placement was tricky, because there was a full-length mirror on the back of the door . . . Oh, well look at that!"

Lidia had just closed the door, and we all turned to see a mirror perfectly reflecting Grandma seated behind the desk. Mi Jin stepped behind Grandma, carefully holding the camera just over her head. Jess backed into a corner, slowly panning over the rest of our faces.

"I gotta say, Edie," Roland said, "I never really got the ending to that movie."

Dad and I exchanged a grin as Grandma sighed.

"You and most critics," she said dryly. "Fortunately, there *are* horror fans out there who can handle a little complexity in their films. Sam, darling, I think you'd *love* it."

Oscar snickered, but Roland looked unfazed. "Enlighten me, then. Was the—"

A soft *thump-thump* cut him off, and we all stared at the door. I did a quick head count; we hadn't left anyone in the hall. The atmosphere in the room shifted immediately. Dad, who was closest to the door, put his hand on the knob and glanced at Jess. She took a few steps closer, her camera trained on him, and nodded. Dad turned the knob and stepped back, allowing the door to drift open.

No one was there.

We all let out a collective breath. "Everyone heard that, right?" Lidia asked softly, and everyone nodded. Sam stepped outside with her, glancing up and down the corridor and frowning. Jess and Roland joined them, and their footsteps faded after a few seconds.

Dad closed the door quietly behind them, then stepped back and waited. Oscar and I stayed silent. We knew the drill; at the first sign of possible paranormal activity, we had to give the ghost enough time to try to communicate again. Mi Jin's camera was still rolling, aimed at the door from her spot behind Grandma.

After nearly two full minutes of dead silence, Dad sighed. "Shall we go see if the others have had any luck?" he asked. Grandma stood, and Mi Jin and Oscar headed for the door. But I stayed in my spot next to the desk, my feet frozen in place.

The Thing was in the mirror. Standing next to the desk, just like me.

Instead of me. Instead of my reflection.

We stared at each other. It smiled. I didn't.

"Kat?" Dad asked, and everyone turned to look at me. "You okay?"

I opened my mouth, unsure of what to say. If they looked in the mirror, would they see it? Or would they see *me*?

But before I could speak, a distant scream sounded from the floor above us.

Mi Jin flew across the room and threw the door open, then took off down the hall, camera still on her shoulder. Grandma and Oscar were right behind her, but Dad waited for me.

"What is it?" he asked, putting his hand on my shoulder.

I forced a smile. "Nothing. Let's go."

We hurried down the hall and up the stairs to the third floor. Just as we reached the top, there was a loud *crash*, followed by lots of shouting and yelling. My heart was pounding out of control as we sprinted down the hall to the source of the noise. Was it the poltergeist? Or had the Thing actually *attacked* someone?

Dad and I had just reached room 313 when Lidia came out, holding someone by the elbow. A girl with long, dark hair, shaking and stammering. For a split second, I went completely numb. Then I recognized her as one of the Talchul Films crew members, the one who looked around Mi Jin's age.

A few doors down, Roland pulled another Talchul person from a room, closely followed by Jess, who was still filming.

"Is Jae-Hwa here?" Lidia asked them calmly. "Does he know you're doing this?"

The girl swallowed and shook her head. The guy Roland had found didn't look nearly as freaked out, but his expression was contrite.

"I'm sorry, I'm so sorry," he kept saying, nervously glancing at the cameras. The rest of the crew had gathered around them in the hall. "Jae-Hwa doesn't know, I promise. We just . . . we thought it would be a more interesting episode, if . . ."

"If you pretended to be the poltergeist," Lidia finished. She didn't sound angry at all, but I could tell by the way her lips were pursed that she was upset. Oscar and I glanced at each other worriedly. "Look, I know you guys need publicity for your movie. But now . . . I don't know if we can use any of the footage we've taken."

Wincing, the guy murmured another apology. Tears streamed silently down the girl's face. But she wasn't looking at Lidia. Instead, she kept glancing toward room 313.

"Hey, it's okay," Grandma said comfortingly. "Yumi, wasn't it? We've still got the rest of the night to film, dear. Don't fret." Yumi swallowed and nodded, her eyes still fixed

171

on the door. Dad glanced at it, then back at her.

"Is something wrong?" he asked.

After a few seconds, Yumi let out a shaky breath. "I saw . . . something."

Silence fell. I saw Roland and Jess exchange a skeptical look, and I couldn't help feeling the same way. After all, these two had just tried to fake us out with soft knocks and screams. But Yumi did seem genuinely upset.

Grandma put a comforting arm around her, and Mi Jin moved closer. "What did you see?"

"A light," Yumi whispered. "In the corner of the room. And something . . . moving."

Dad pushed open the door and glanced inside. "Room 313 . . . this is the room with the portal sightings, right?" He turned to Lidia. "We were planning on spending some time in here, anyway," he told her. "Maybe we can get started while you give Jae-Hwa a call?"

Lidia nodded, gesturing for Yumi and the other guy to follow her. The rest of the crew traipsed inside room 313. Oscar and I lingered behind in the hallway for a moment.

"Do you think she was lying?" I whispered, glancing at Yumi as she disappeared into the stairwell.

Oscar shrugged. "Dunno. She sure looked freaked out. But she could just be a really good actor." He paused. "Speaking of . . . what happened downstairs? Right before we heard that scream?"

Avoiding his gaze, I pulled the Elapse out of my

pocket and hung it around my neck. I should've told them downstairs, pointed to the Thing in the mirror so everyone could've seen. But it was too late now. I wasn't even sure Oscar would believe me. "Oh, nothing."

"Yeah, you know who *isn't* a good actor?" Oscar said. "You. Come on, Kat. What did you—"

"Kat? Oscar?" Dad called, and I hurried inside room 313 before Oscar could finish the question.

CHAPTER SEVENTEEN
THE LIGHT AT THE END OF THE TUNNEL

In: DRAFTS
From: acciopancakes@mymail.net
To: monicam@mymail.net
Subject: I'm coming home

Dear Mother,
I'm so sorry for everything. Now I'm ready to be the daughter you've always wanted. The old Kat will be gone soon, and then you and I can be together forever.
Love,
Kat

"**No.**" Roland leaned against the wall next to Sam, hands in his pockets. "Do we air all of that nonsense, or not?"

Jess set her camera down on the bed and sighed. "I don't know. I mean, it's the season finale, and what do we have—a few kids sneaking around, knocking on doors and running away?"

"Well, like Edie said, we've got the rest of the night to film." Dad frowned thoughtfully. "And to be honest, I think maybe that could be a great way to start the episode. Outing the fake stuff right away, even before the first commercial break. It might give us more credibility with the more skeptical fans, you know?"

"Good point." Jess made a face. "Although I have to admit, this makes me wonder how much of what they told us yesterday is actually true. All the stories about the poltergeist, the portal . . ."

Sam ran his fingers over the wallpaper, moving to the far left corner. "This room does have a different energy than the others," he mused. "Seems chillier, too."

Roland rummaged around in his bag and pulled out his thermal camera attachment, which he slid onto his phone. Mi Jin moved over to stand just behind him as he turned it on, angling her camera to see the screen on his phone. I stepped back so I could see, too. Sam's outline glowed yellow and green against a background of various blues and purples. Roland moved closer to the corner Sam had been inspecting, Mi Jin right on his heels.

"Huh," he murmured, kneeling on the floor. "That's interesting."

The rest of us gathered behind him to see. The corner itself looked totally normal: light blue-green wallpaper, bright white tiled floor. But the thermal image showed something . . . else. A brief, yellowish something that vanished when Roland shifted the camera's position, then reappeared when he shifted it back. He stood slowly, scanning the corner from the floor up to the ceiling. The yellowish aura slipped in and out of view, like a fog seeping in where the two walls met.

"Perhaps Yumi really did see something here," Grandma said at last, breaking the silence. "She said there was a light moving in the corner, right?"

"Yeah." Roland lowered his phone and gestured at the walls. "But I'm not seeing anything unusual without the thermal camera. You?" The last question was directed at Sam, who was already tracing his fingers across the wallpaper. He stared and stared, brow furrowed, like the wall was a foggy window and he was trying to see what was on the other side.

While Mi Jin continued to film them, Jess turned her camera on Dad and Grandma, and they quickly slipped back into hosting mode. "What was it Jae-Hwa told us yesterday?" Dad asked. "That former patients and staff have claimed to see a bright light in this room?"

Grandma nodded. "Like a light at the end of a tunnel," she recited. "Which is why this room was so unpopular with patients, and often vacant. It's unclear whether they thought the room itself was haunted, or the patients who stayed in this room were cursed themselves."

While they continued talking, I wandered around the room, mentally framing a few shots. I was itching to take a few photos, but I didn't want the Elapse making everyone feel disoriented and anxious. Its residual haunting effect seemed to have less power the more people were around, like in the elevator back at the Montgomery. Still, not worth the risk.

Room 313 looked pretty much like every other room we'd been in on the second floor: small, neatly made bed against the back wall, simple dresser with mirror on the left wall, a steel cabinet stocked with tissues, boxes of rubber gloves, jars of tongue depressors, and other medical equipment. I eyed the mirror nervously, half expecting to see the Thing looking back at me. To my relief, my reflection was completely normal; cropped hair, jeans, and the black *Final Girl Productions* hoodie Grandma had given me before we left the hotel.

We stayed in the room for another fifteen minutes, but Roland's thermal camera had stopped showing the yellowish aura and I could tell Jess was getting restless. Her phone buzzed, and she fished it out of her pocket with her free hand while balancing the camera on her shoulder. She glanced at the screen, and her eyes lit up.

"It's Lidia," she told us, already heading for the door. "Cafeteria, *now.*"

Quickly, I flipped on the Elapse as everyone hurried into the hall, ignoring the way my heart immediately started pounding out of control. Now that the small room was empty, I wanted to get a picture of the supposed portal-corner for myself. Oscar hovered in the doorway.

"Kat, come on!"

"Right behind you!" I said. "Just want to get this one shot . . ."

I turned the Elapse vertical so I could capture the whole

corner from top to bottom, then adjusted the focus. Then I snapped the photo, and two things happened at once:

The door clicked closed, very softly.

The fluorescent bulbs flickered, then went out.

I froze, still gazing at the viewfinder. Because even though the lights had gone out, the room wasn't dark. A thin line of light had appeared in the corner, like there was a crack running from the floor to the ceiling. As I watched, it grew wider and wider until it was roughly the size of a doorway. And on the other side, as if at the end of a very, very long tunnel, stood a girl-shaped shadow.

When I lowered my camera, the tunnel was still there.

I didn't hesitate. I didn't even think about what I was doing.

I shielded my eyes and stepped inside.

CHAPTER EIGHTEEN
DOCTOR PAIN WILL SEE YOU NOW

WARNING! Recording Mode Is Unavailable In This Format

MY eyelids were no match for the blinding brightness. No matter how hard I squeezed my eyes closed, I could still see the neon pink of the insides of my lids. I could practically *smell* the light—a sharp, antiseptic scent way more intense than the vaguely bleach-like smell in the rest of the hospital. My skin prickled in a way that reminded me of my encounter with Sonja Hillebrandt back in Crimptown, when the air had suddenly shifted and I'd felt like I'd walked into a cloud of static electricity.

I kept walking, covering my eyes with one arm and waving the other, trying to find the wall and groping nothing instead. After what felt like forever, I thought I noticed the light begin to fade and I slowed to a halt. Hesitantly, I dropped my arm, then squinted around.

I was standing in the corner of room 313, facing the room. But everything was . . . reversed. Like the negative of a color photo. The white tiled floor was pitch-black, and the light blue-green wallpaper was bloodred. The room was flipped, too, like a reflection—the shelves and the dresser had swapped walls, the door was opposite the bed. Distantly, I heard a muffled ringing sound, like a fire alarm going off in the building next door. Behind me, the portal in the corner glowed white.

But as weird as all of that was, it barely registered in my brain. Because the Thing was standing in the middle of the room. Head tilted, blinking at me curiously. Then it spoke.

"She."

I stood there dumbly, half convinced I was hallucinating. "What?"

"You always call me *it*," the Thing said. "A *thing*. But I'm a girl. More of a girl than you are."

The insult took a few seconds to sink in. I was too distracted by hearing the sound of my own voice, but all twisted and warped. Despite the cruel words, the Thing spoke softly and sweetly, like a little girl. And there was a weird distance, too. It was hard to explain, but it kind of sounded like a recording, despite the fact that it was right here in the room with me.

"You aren't a girl," I said finally, trying to sound confident. "You aren't a *person*. You're something I created, and I'll call you whatever I want." Hearing the way my own voice shook forced me to realize what I'd been attempting to ignore.

I was *terrified*.

In the last four months, I'd dealt with plenty of scary stuff. Emily and her knife and her high-pitched laugh. Lidia when she was possessed by a dead angry pirate. The ghosts of electrocuted prisoners and lost, frightened campers and even a possessed nun who'd never actually existed as a human being, but did as a paranormal being.

But the Thing was different. It wasn't exactly ghost, and it wasn't exactly human. It wasn't even a doppelganger. It was an actual part of me, a part I'd spent most of my life trying to ignore.

"You didn't create me," the Thing said in a singsong way that raised goose bumps up and down my arms. "You *hid* me. You hid me from my mother. All you had to do was let me out, and she never ever would have left us."

I shook my head, but tears were already streaming down my face. "That's not true."

"It is." The Thing sighed. "You made us wear that *Bride of Frankenstein* shirt in our sixth-grade school photo just to make her mad. You whined every time she asked if she could paint our nails or do our hair. You pouted every time she took us shopping." It took a step forward, its eyes flashing. "Why did you have to push her away? She was just trying to spend time with us."

"She was trying to *change* me," I said weakly, wiping my eyes. "She was trying to make me . . . you."

The Thing stamped its foot. "I *am* you!" it roared, and suddenly its voice wasn't girly and sweet anymore. "All you had to do was let me out! And we'd all be happy! Mom and Dad would still be together, we'd be a family, we'd have a normal life instead of *this*. We don't even have a *house* anymore, we live in hotels and stay in abandoned prisons and hospitals and Dad *wants* to go back to our home in Chelsea and you won't—"

"He does *not*!" I shouted, suddenly furious. "He loves our life now, he's just . . . he's scared he's not being a good father. Mostly thanks to *you*. But a miserable life isn't a normal life, and we were *all* miserable—Mom, Dad, me. It didn't matter that we were all in a house together. Everyone's happier with the way things are now, even Mom."

"Happier with her new daughter," the Thing sneered. "Don't you see? If she wasn't happy with you, it's *your* fault."

I closed my eyes. I knew that was wrong. I'd known ever since Grandma and Dad had told me Mom backed out on coming out to see me. *She can be very, very selfish.* It was true that I could have tried harder with Mom. I could have talked to her on the phone when she called after moving to Cincinnati. I could have swallowed my complaints when she took me shopping or painted my nails.

But she could have tried harder, too. She could have taken me to play laser tag when we'd passed it on our way to the mall. She could have helped me with my vampire Elsa makeup in seventh grade instead of sighing and asking if I was *sure* I wouldn't rather be regular Elsa for Halloween instead.

I'd gone bridesmaid dress shopping with her over Thanksgiving, I'd had dinners and watched movies with her and Anthony and Elena, and I was going to her wedding shower in a few weeks. She could have come to Seoul. She could have taken an interest in my new life, like I was trying to do with hers.

I *knew* all this. It was time to actually believe it.

"It's her fault, too," I whispered, my eyes still closed. "I'm trying now. But she still isn't, not really. Maybe she will someday, but until then, there's nothing else I can do."

"Of course there is," the Thing said, all soft and sweet again. "You can change who you are. Look how easy it is!"

I opened my eyes and took a step back. "What the . . ."

No more dress, no more braid. The Thing had my short ponytail, my *Final Girl* hoodie and jeans. It really was my doppelganger now.

"I knew you wouldn't be willing to do what it takes to fix our family," the Thing told me. "That's why I brought you here. You entered the portal, but I'm the one who's leaving."

And then it leaped forward and shoved me hard into the shelf before sprinting across the room to the portal.

CHAPTER NINETEEN
HELLO FROM THE OTHER SIDE

P2P WIKI
Entry: "Out-of-body experience"
[Last edited by Maytrix]

An out-of-body experience occurs when a person feels their soul, essence, or spirit has stepped out of their body. In extreme cases, some claim to actually see their physical body from this outside point of view. Out-of-body experiences are often induced by trauma and can occcur simultaneously with near-death experiences.

THE shelf rocked back against the wall as I slid to the floor. One bottle fell, then another, both smashing on the black tile. I tried to scramble to my feet, but the shelf tilted forward precariously, raining down more glass bottles and sharp metal instruments. A heavy cylinder hit my head, and bright spots danced in front of my eyes. I grabbed at the shelf again, this time to steady myself, but missed and landed hard on my hands and knees. Shards of glass sliced my palms, but I ignored the pain and got to my feet.

The Thing stood right in front of the portal. It smiled.

"Five seconds."

But the voice didn't come from either of us. It was distant, almost like it was coming from an intercom. The portal started to flicker, and the Thing turned to step inside.

I'd never reach it in time. Without thinking, I grabbed the Elapse from around my neck and hurled it at the Thing. It smacked into the back of its head, and the Thing stumbled. I lunged across the room and seized its hair and *pulled*.

"Five seconds."

The Thing screamed, struggling to turn and face me with its head bent backward. I saw the Elapse on the floor just before the Thing stomped on it with a sickening crunch. A fresh wave of anger coursed through me, and using all my remaining strength, I shoved the Thing away from the portal as hard as I could. Then, ignoring its shrieks of anger, I threw myself inside.

I felt its fingers graze my ankle and tug desperately before I slipped out of its grasp. The screams quickly faded to nothing.

The light was even more intense this time. I crossed both arms over my eyes, wincing at the stings from the cuts on my hands.

"Just five seconds."

"What . . ." I mumbled, and the grogginess of my own voice startled me. I needed to stop running before I crashed into something. Except . . . except I wasn't running. I was lying down. On . . . nothing.

I was floating.

The light dimmed, and I lowered my arms. I was looking down at room 313, back to normal now with white floors and blue-green wallpaper instead of black and red. The corner was just a regular corner, no sign of a portal or anything unusual.

And Oscar was there, kneeling on the floor next to someone. Someone unconscious.

Me.

Panic seized me. Had the Thing somehow made it out of the portal? *That's not me!* I tried to yell, but I couldn't make a sound. Then I noticed blood on the girl's hands, and I relaxed. The Thing hadn't made it out. It was me on the floor.

That's a weird thing to feel relieved about, said a voice in my head. *You do look kind of dead. And it's not a good sign that you're up here watching yourself, is it?*

That's true, I agreed. *I should go back down there.*

As soon as I had the thought, everything went dark. I felt heavy, all of a sudden, like my bones had turned to concrete.

"I don't know what happened, I left her alone for just five seconds!"

Oscar's panicked voice was suddenly very close. I realized my eyes were closed, and struggled to open them. His face swam in my vision, his worried expression quickly changing to relieved when I focused on him.

"She's awake!"

Another face was there, and another . . . too many. Dad, Grandma, the whole crew. No cameras, at least not pointed at me—both hung limp at Jess's and Mi Jin's sides. Everyone seemed to be talking at once, hands feeling my forehead, pulling me up into a sitting position, bracing my back when I slumped over.

"What happened?"

"Is that blood?"

"Her hands—Mi Jin, get the first aid kit!"

"Did you fall?"

"Did you hit your head?"

I blinked slowly, trying to get my thoughts in order. "No, I didn't . . . I'm fine, I just . . ."

"Okay!" Grandma said loudly, and everyone else fell silent. "Let's give her a little space, shall we?" She helped me up and led me over to the bed, sitting down next to me as Lidia handed her the first aid kid. "Where on earth did these cuts come from?"

"Glass," I mumbled. "Some bottles fell off the shelf."

Grandma glanced at the shelf, where the jars and instruments still sat undisturbed. "Mmhmm," was all she said. Then she smiled up at Jess. "Mind if I sit here with my granddaughter for a bit? The rest of you really should get down to the cafeteria and find Lidia."

She said it kindly, but there was no hint of a question in her voice. Jess hedged for a moment, tapping her fingers on the side of her camera.

"Yeah, of course. You sure you're okay, Kat?"

I nodded. "Yeah, I'm fine."

Jess smiled, then headed back out into the hall. The rest of the crew followed, although Oscar looked pretty reluctant to leave. Dad stayed by the bed, watching as Grandma opened a tube of antibiotic cream.

"You should get down there, too, Jack," she said without looking up. "She'll be fine."

"I'm okay," I added, doing my best to sound normal despite the grogginess that still lingered. "Totally fine. It's just a few scratches. I was taking a few photos when the light went out, and I tripped and fell."

Dad sighed, and I felt a sinking feeling in my stomach. I was lying again, and he knew it. I had to stop doing this. I was only making things worse.

"Actually, that's not true." My heart pounded faster, but I forced myself to say it. "The truth is . . . the doppelganger we saw on the bridge was here. It's not a doppelganger, though, not exactly. It's an artificial ghost I made. Like Brunilda Cano. But it's like a version of me that . . . that Mom would like better. It ripped up your contract and left those messages on Mom's Facebook, all of that stuff. And tonight, when you guys left the room, I stayed just to take a few photos, and it . . . attacked me."

"*Attacked* you?"

"The portal in the corner," I said hurriedly, wanting to get this over with, fully aware of how ridiculous it sounded.

"It opened, and I went in, and that's when it pushed me into the shelf—the other shelf, in the other room 313. It was trying to come back here, to replace me."

My breaths were coming quick and short now. I chanced a peek at Dad's face, then Grandma's. Dad's brow was furrowed, but Grandma looked perfectly serene. Neither looked ready to lock me up, so that was something.

"The reason I didn't tell you any of this before is that I figured you'd think I was crazy," I finished. "But it's the truth."

"Kat, honey . . ." Dad sat down on my other side, the bed creaking beneath the weight of all three of us. "I would never think that. I'm glad you're finally being honest with me."

I looked up at him in surprise. "You believe me?"

He started to respond, then pressed his lips together thoughtfully. "I can tell when you're lying," he said finally. "And you're not. But I'll admit, everything you just said is kind of . . ."

"True," Grandma finished. Dad and I both looked at her in surprise. "Well, Jack, look at these cuts on her hands. Do you see any glass, anything in this room that could've done this to her? And, KitKat, you said you were taking photos, but I can't help noticing you don't seem to have your camera."

My heart twisted as the image of the broken Elapse lying on the black tiled floor surfaced in my mind. "I lost it," I whispered. "It's in the other room 313."

Dad stood and walked slowly around the room, peering under the bed and around the sides of the shelf. Then he sat next to me again, his face a bit pale.

Grandma chuckled. "Well, I'm sorry," she said when Dad gave her a funny look. "But you *are* the host of a ghost-hunters show whose motto is *Believe.* So . . . can't you?"

"I . . . well . . . yes, of course I can," Dad said, shaking his head. "But I'm just trying to . . ." He turned to me. "Kat, I thought I didn't understand what was going on with you over the last few weeks. But it seems like maybe I haven't understood what you've been going through over the last few *years.* And that's what really scares me."

"I'm sorry." Tears welled up in my eyes, and I brushed them away. "I thought I could fix this by myself. I thought if I told you what was going on, you'd think you were right about putting me in danger."

Dad opened his mouth, but I cut him off. "And yeah, okay, so I did get hurt tonight. But the Thing has been real to me since I was like *eight.* It's always haunted me, even back in Chelsea. What happened just now has nothing to do with the show, I swear. It . . . it was going to happen no matter what. I had to face it."

I was breathing heavily by now, and Grandma put a supportive hand on my back. Dad rubbed his forehead wearily, looking from me to the corner.

"So this . . . *thing,*" he said finally. "You said it's a different version of yourself that your . . . your mother would prefer over you?" His voice broke a little.

"Yeah." I smiled tightly. "It's hard to explain."

"I'm listening."

"But Jess is probably waiting for you," I said. "They're filming, you should—"

"Kat," Dad interrupted gently. "They can film without me for a few minutes. Tell me everything."

So I took a deep, shaky breath.

And I started from the beginning.

Post: So Here's the Thing [Vlog]
Comments (367)
[Transcript]

Hi, everyone! Kat Sinclair here. I started typing out a long post about the whole doppelganger thing, but then Oscar suggested I do a vlog instead. Which I . . . well, I really didn't want to do, because in case it isn't obvious, I hate being on camera. But sometimes facing your fears is a good thing, so . . . here goes.

On my first day with *Passport to Paranormal*, Roland told me making the show was a no-win situation. If they found proof of paranormal activity, people would say they faked it. If they did fake something, people would get mad—like the exploding lightbulb in the first episode. And if they did nothing, well, you guys might think the show was boring.

Turns out running this blog is kind of the same. I've posted photos and videos on here of what I believed was evidence of paranormal activity. Some were real. Some turned out to be different from what I thought they were. But I didn't fake any of them. I know some of you will never believe me, and that's okay. But I promise I've never lied on my blog.

And I'm still a skeptic. Most of the time, when something that might seem paranormal happens, there's a logical reason for it. But not always.

This should be the part where I explain exactly what's been

going on the last few weeks. I know my behavior has seemed a little weird . . . and that's a nicer way of putting it than a lot of you guys in the comments. There's a reason for it. And yeah, it's a paranormal one.

But I'm not going to talk about it.

Because it's personal. And because I know not everyone will believe it. And others will say I'm just doing it for attention, or it's publicity for the show. It's hard, because I want to defend my dad from fans, and supposedly "professional" reporters, who claim he's a bad father.

Here's what I will say about the last few weeks: The doppelganger you saw in the Yongheng Bridge episode was real. It left comments on the *P2P* forums and other places online pretending to be me. It did show up in the Ryang Psychiatric Hospital when we were filming the finale, and it did try to hurt me, but I'm fine. And it's . . . well, I'm not sure where it is now. But I haven't seen it since.

But you won't see any of that. In fact, you won't see my dad or me much at all in the second half of the episode, because he was busy taking care of me. He's a great host, but he's an even better dad.

Here's another thing Roland told me my first day: The reason people are drawn to Sam Sumners is that he's haunted. And you know what I realized? We're all haunted by something. You probably are, too, if you're a fan of a ghost-hunters show. We all have secrets, skeletons in our closets, things that follow us no matter how hard we try to forget about them. Maybe they're paranormal and maybe they're not, but to the person they're following, they're real. Sam knows this, and that's what makes him such a great medium. It's not really about communicating with spirits. It's about listening to people who are ready to talk about who or what is haunting them. And it's about believing them, even if they don't have "proof."

That's what I've learned since I joined *Passport to Paranormal*. And I'm looking forward to helping more people—

and ghosts—move on next season, and telling you all about their stories right here on *The Kat Sinclair Files*.

Whether or not you believe is up to you.

OSCAR and I filmed the video for my last blog post of the season the day after the Ryang investigation. Dad approved it right away, and I published it. Then I closed the laptop and spent the rest of the afternoon with Oscar.

We went back to the market and bought "Heart and Seoul" T-shirts for Jamie and Hailey. We drank two giant bubble teas each, then found an arcade with Dance Dance Revolution to help us burn off the sugar rush. We spent almost two hours walking on the stone path of the beautiful old fortress just a few blocks from our hotel, talking about summer, Oscar's next therapy session with Roland, my mom, his dad, Trish and Mark, Thiago, and basically anything other than *the* Thing and what had happened in room 313. Until we found a little bench overlooking the small park inside the fortress and sat, and Oscar said:

"I knew something was wrong this time."

I glanced at him. "This time?"

"Yeah, in room 313." Oscar exhaled, and I could see his breath in the chilly air. "After I left you in there, I was almost to the stairs when I felt . . . déjà vu. Like I was back in Daems, right before Emily jumped out of that cell. Except this time, I knew something bad was about to happen."

"Oh." I waited, watching him squeeze his gloved hands

into fists, then flex his fingers, over and over. Squeeze, flex. Squeeze, flex.

"So I ran back to the room, and . . ."

"Found me on the floor," I finished. "You were right."

"No." Oscar shook his head. "I mean, yes, I was right. But you weren't on the floor."

"What?"

He looked at me. "You were standing in the corner. Really, really still, like a statue. It freaked me out, so I called your name, and . . . and you started falling over. You almost fell into the shelf, but I caught you."

My mouth fell open. "Seriously? That's . . . I don't remember that." I paused, picturing the scene he'd described. "Do you think . . . do you think all of that stuff in the other room 313 happened in my head?"

"No."

I rolled my eyes. "Oscar, come on. You don't have to pretend—"

"Your camera," he interrupted. "I saw you taking pictures right before I left, then five seconds later I came back in and you weren't holding it anymore. And there's those cuts on your hands, too. Maybe when I walked back into room 313, it was right when you walked *out* of the other one. I don't know. But whatever happened, you went . . . somewhere."

I pulled off one of my mittens and studied the bandages on my palm, remembering how hard the Thing had shoved me, the way the shelf had rocked back and forth, sending the bottles crashing down on me. Then I looked up at Oscar.

"I could have really gotten hurt," I told him. "If you hadn't shown up, and I'd fallen into the shelf—the real one. It could've been a lot worse than a few cuts on my hands." When he shrugged, I nudged him with my elbow. "No, seriously. You said you keep replaying the Emily thing because you should've reacted faster when she attacked us. Like you should've known something was wrong before it happened. And this time . . . you did."

Oscar smiled a little. "Yeah, I guess that's true."

"Thank you," I said. He rolled his eyes, but I could tell he was pleased.

"You're welcome."

Once the sun had set, we headed back to the hotel and arrived just as Lidia and Roland showed up carrying several bags of takeout. We went up to Lidia's room and spread out a buffet on the desk: different kinds of spicy pork and chicken, sticky rice, pickled vegetables, and tons of kimchi. Mi Jin put on *Return to the Asylum,* and Grandma entertained everyone with her commentary, inserting behind-the-scenes anecdotes and adding inappropriate punch lines whenever her character spoke. Jess kept giggling at Dad, who struggled with his metal chopsticks and finally gave up, using one like a fork to stab his chicken. Sam loved the movie, to Grandma's delight, and she immediately put in the DVD of the prequel when the first one was finished.

We were almost to the part where Grandma's character

knocks out a nurse and steals her uniform when Dad caught my eye and pointed to the clock on the nightstand. "Almost nine," he mouthed, and I nodded.

Oscar followed me out, but neither of us spoke until we were in the hall. "The first one was good, but I don't know about the second one," Oscar said as we headed to me and Dad's room. "How can she play the Warden? The Warden was the villain who killed her character in the first movie!"

"Yeah, a lot of people really hated that," I said with a grin. "It only makes sense if the first movie was all a hallucination in the Warden's head."

"So weird." Oscar shook his head, following me into the room. "Hey, what's that?"

He pointed to a familiar zombie snowman gift bag sitting on my bed. I grinned as I picked it up and flipped over the tag.

KitKat,
Try not to take this one into the spirit realm, okay?
Love, Grandma

Oscar peered at the note. "Ooh, new camera?"

"I think so," I said, pulling the box out of the bag. *Elapse E-500* was printed across the top in bright yellow letters, along with a ton of words in Hangul. Eagerly, I ripped off the tape sealing the lid. "It's the latest model! How'd she get it so fast?"

"Mi Jin mentioned an electronics market not far from here," Oscar said. "Your grandma must've gone there this morning."

A sudden beeping melody caused us both to jump.

"Well, here goes nothing." I handed Oscar the Elapse and hurried over to the laptop. A message on the screen read: *Accept video chat from MonicaMills?* I clicked *Yes*, and a moment later, my mom's face filled the screen.

"Kat!"

"Hi, Mom." I smiled back at her, then waved when a pair of bright eyes peered over her shoulder. "Hi, Elena."

"Elena, sweetie, eat your breakfast," Mom said, turning away to lift my future stepsister and plop her into her booster seat. "Sorry about that. So!" She leaned forward and gave me an expectant smile. "How's Seoul? Were you excited to see your grandmother?"

"Yeah, really surprised." I glanced in the mirror at Oscar's reflection. He was lying on the bed, pretending to examine the Elapse but eyeing my mom curiously. "We're having lots of fun. It's, um . . . it's too bad you couldn't make it."

Mom's face tightened a little, confirming my suspicion that she'd been hoping Dad and Grandma wouldn't tell me that she was supposed to come, too. I wondered how many little secrets they'd kept from me in the last thirteen years to protect Mom, and waited to feel the familiar wave of anger at her. But it didn't come. I just felt disappointed and sad.

And kind of sorry for her. That was . . . new.

"Yes, well," Mom said, leaning over to pick up a spoon Elena had dropped. "I'm so sorry about that, but it's just been crazy here lately, you know?"

"Yeah." I shrugged. "It's fine."

"So Grandma tells me you and your father might be moving back into the old house?" Mom asked lightly. "I bet Trish and Mark will be thrilled to have you back!"

"Actually, Dad and I talked about that this morning." I took a deep breath. "We're going to sell it."

Mom's eyes widened. "Oh? He and I talked last week, and he said he was leaning toward taking a job in Cincinnati."

"He turned it down. He said he'd call you tomorrow," I added quickly, "but that it was okay for me to tell you. He's staying with the show."

"Oh! That's . . ." Mom's phone buzzed, vibrating next to Elena's cereal bowl. She glanced at it, tapped at the screen, then smiled at me again. "That's great! I bet you're excited. But you've both got a few months off until you start filming the next season, right?"

"Yeah." I shifted in my chair. "We're going to stay with Grandma until after your wedding, then, we're, uh . . . we're going to L.A. with her."

"That'll be a fun trip!"

"No, it's not a trip, not exactly." I bit my lip, trying not to laugh at the sight of Oscar's reflection doing a happy dance, waving his arms and bouncing up and down on the bed.

"We're going to look at apartments. Or houses. Just to see if we'd like it there."

My heart thumped as I watched my mother's face carefully. I wasn't sure what kind of reaction I expected, or wanted. Dad and I had decided this morning that if he was going to stay with *Passport to Paranormal*, we still needed a home base—but that could be anywhere. And it wasn't Chelsea, not anymore. I'd still miss Trish and Mark, but they were my online best friends now. My real-life best friend was right behind me, pulling silent, ridiculous faces at me in the mirror. (He'd looked up train tickets between Los Angeles and Portland, where he lived with Lidia, the second I told him about L.A., much to Dad and Lidia's amusement.)

The only thing that still made Chelsea feel like home was Grandma. And she was moving to L.A. to start filming her production company's first movie. If Dad and I were going to try to find a new home base, we agreed it was as good a place to start as any.

Of course, I wouldn't see Mom nearly as often as I would if we moved back to Chelsea. Part of me wanted her to acknowledge that. Maybe even be a little upset about it. Tell me she'd miss me too much to live halfway across the country from me and beg me to reconsider.

But she just brushed her bangs out of her eyes and smiled. "L.A., wow! How are you feeling about that?"

"Pretty excited," I replied. It was a massive understatement. "You've been a few times, right?"

Mom nodded. "With Grandma, when I was little. Loved it—we did all the touristy stuff, Disneyland, everything. I bet it's changed a lot, though."

"You can come visit us." I kept my voice carefully light. "It'd be fun!"

"Of course I will!" Mom said brightly. "As soon as Anthony and I get back from Cancún, we'll start planning a trip out there."

And that was it. No protests, no pleading. She was fine with her daughter traveling the world and living in another state. She had Anthony and Elena and a whole new life, and for right now, I only fit in with e-mails and video chats and the occasional visit. That was how much she was willing to try.

Which was fine. Because now I could see the difference between Dad and Mom clearly. They'd both made mistakes—and so had I—but Dad always put me first. Mom put *herself* first.

And that wasn't my fault.

Mom and I talked for another fifteen minutes, mostly about a photo shoot she'd just done for the zoo. I told her about the thoughtography exhibit I'd gone to with Jamie, and she laughed and rolled her eyes, just like I knew she would. The horror-loving gene must have skipped Mom somehow, because she was never into paranormal stuff like Grandma and I were.

After we said goodbye, I twisted around in my chair.

"Hey, mind if I . . ." I trailed off when I realized Oscar was snoring. He was sprawled on his back, the Elapse lying on the comforter next to him. Smiling, I turned back to the laptop and logged into my e-mail.

From: acciopancakes@mymail.net
To: timelord2002@mymail.net, trishhhhbequiet@mymail.net
Subject: Re: Re: That blog post

Hey!! Sorry about that last e-mail. It's a LOOOOONG story but I swear all the weird "Real Kat Sinclair" drama is over. I'd rather tell you about it in person in a few weeks. Can't wait to see you guys!
<3 Kat

From: acciopancakes@mymail.net
To: jamiebaggins@mymail.net
Subject: doppelgangers are the WORST

I don't know if you read my last blog post yet but OMG. You won't believe what happened at Ryang. Actually, you WILL believe it, because you believe everything paranormal. Even when it's totally ridiculous (and sometimes fake). :)
Can we video chat sometime this week so I can tell you about it? Hailey, too! I'll give you a preview:
1. My doppelganger totally attacked me
2. In a freaking PORTAL
3. I'm pretty sure I had an actual out-of-body experience (I looked it up on the *P2P* Wiki)
<3 Kat
PS: Dad's in for next season
PPS: We're going to look for apartments in L.A.
PPPS: There's a pretty cool-looking cemetery in Hollywood that

would be great for an episode of *Graveyard Slot*. Or a third date. ;)

I started to close the laptop, then opened my blog instead. I stared at the video, but didn't hit play. I'd already watched it with Dad right before I posted it. My hands hadn't even started sweating at the sight of myself on the screen, which I guess was progress. There were 237 comments pending, so I logged into my dashboard and started scrolling through, clicking *Approve* next to each one. As usual, most of the commenters were from the *P2P* forums, although I'd gained several new followers, too. Their comments ranged from support to confusion to disbelief, but nothing rude or trollish. Then I got to the last one.

xFxLxAxIxLxxGxRxIxNx
welcome 2 california. ghosts love the sun.

After a moment's hesitation, I clicked on the username. A new tab opened to a white page with *Error 404* on the top left. Below, letters began to appear, as if someone was typing.

we'll be waiting, Kat.

Then the browser closed, and I was staring at the desktop covered in Dad's folders.

"Oookay . . ." I reopened the browser and logged back into my dashboard. The comment was gone.

After a few seconds, I closed the laptop and tiptoed over to the bed. Picking up the Elapse, I sat down gingerly next to Oscar. This was probably the first time he'd slept soundly in the last few weeks.

So I examined the Elapse as quietly as I could. It had a few new features, but otherwise looked and felt just like the one Grandma had given me right before Dad and I had left Chelsea.

I hadn't wanted to admit it then, but we'd been running away. Both of us. Living in the same house after Mom left had been hard. Everything reminded me of the way our lives had been *before*, and I knew it must have been the same for Dad. *Passport to Paranormal* had been our escape. And at some point—I wasn't sure when, Brussels? Salvador?—the show had become our new life, and I'd stopped wishing for things to go back to the way they had been.

Things were different now. We were still with the show, but we weren't running away anymore.

We were moving on.

"Dontaympisher," Oscar mumbled, and I snickered.

"What?"

He squinted up at me, his eye bloodshot. "Don't take my picture."

"I wasn't going to." I pointed the Elapse at the ceiling. "No offense, but you could use some more beauty sleep."

"Mmph." Oscar rubbed his face, then stared at the camera, looking a little more alert. "Did I miss anything? Take any videos of creepy girls in the mirror?"

I snorted. "No. Although I got a creepy comment on my blog."

Oscar sat up. "A troll?"

"No, just something about California having ghosts." I paused. "That are waiting for me, apparently."

"That's weird." Oscar wrinkled his nose. "Wait . . . you didn't say anything about moving to L.A. on your blog yet, right?"

"Nope."

"So how did . . ."

I grinned. "No idea. So what should my first picture be?"

"Huh?"

Lowering the Elapse, I aimed the viewfinder at the TV and shrugged. "New camera, you know? I guess I feel like the first picture I take with it should be important."

"Oh." Oscar was silent for a moment. "We could go back to that fortress tomorrow morning. Or walk to the river. Or . . . didn't Mi Jin mention something about an observation deck?"

"Yeah." I thought about it, turning the Elapse over and over in my hands. "Actually . . . how about this?" I held the camera up with one hand, aiming the lens at us, and pressed the side of my head against Oscar's. I scrunched up my nose and stuck out my tongue, and I knew without looking that Oscar was making a goofy face, too.

Click!